# Wild Ride on Bigfoot Mountain

# #6

# Wild Ride on Bigfoot Mountain

# Paul Buchanan
## Created by Paul Buchanan and Rod Randall

BROADMAN
& HOLMAN
PUBLISHERS

Nashville, Tennessee

0–8054–1975–6

Published by Broadman & Holman Publishers, Nashville, Tennessee
Editorial Team: Vicki Crumpton, Janis Whipple, Kim Overcash
Page Composition: SL Editorial Services

Dewey Decimal Classification: Fiction
Subject Heading: CHRISTIAN FICTION—JUVENILE FICTION
Library of Congress Card Catalog Number: 99–23223

All Scripture quotations are from The Holy Bible, New International Version (NIV) © 1973, 1978, 1984 International Bible Society; used by permission.

**Library of Congress Cataloging-in-Publication Data**
Buchanan, Paul, 1959
      Wild ride on Bigfoot Mountain / Paul Buchanan.
          p.        cm.—(Heebie Jeebies series ; bk. 6)
      Summary: Thirteen-year-old Erich asks for God's protection when he and his best friend Riley uncover a strange skeleton and find evidence of a monster living in the woods near Erich's house.
      ISBN 0–8054–1975–6 (pb)
      [1. Best friends Fiction. 2. Friendship Fiction. 3. Horror stories. 4. Christian life Fiction.] I. Title. II. Series: Heebie Jeebies series ; v. 6.
PZ7.B87717Wi    1999
[Fic]—dc21                             99-23223
                                            CIP

1 2 3 4 5 03 02 01 00 99

# DEDICATION

For Austin Holm

# Chapter 1

First of all, let me tell you about where I live. What's the first thing I see when I look out my bedroom window every morning? Pine trees. What do I pass every day on my way home from school? Pine trees. What do I see when I step out of church every Sunday morning? Pine trees. What keeps sprouting out of our front lawn if I forget to mow it? Pine trees. What completely surrounds the little town I live in? No surprise here—pine trees.

Most of us in McCreeville, Washington, don't even get Christmas trees during the holidays—inside the house is about the only place we can get away from them. Not that I have anything against trees. It's just that I live deep in the forest, and it's pretty easy to get tired of the smell of pines and the dark shadows they cast over everything. So I wasn't terribly upset last spring when a logging truck and

1

a couple of bulldozers rumbled into town and cut down a few acres of pines right behind my house.

After school, my best friend, Riley Hope, and I went out and sat on my back steps with a big bag of chocolate chip cookies, and we watched the bulldozers level the ground and tear up the tree stumps. In a town as boring as McCreeville, this passes for top-notch entertainment. Believe it or not, the hottest activity for the kids in this town is *shuffleboard*.

"Maybe they're building a baseball diamond," Riley said hopefully. "Or maybe a football field or something."

I looked over at Riley. He had cookie crumbs all over his T-shirt. He's the same age as me, thirteen, but he's at least a foot taller and probably twenty pounds heavier. He must eat twice his weight in food every day. He's pretty cool, but sometimes he seems to live in his own little world. He teases me about being a good student and getting A's on all my book reports, and I tease him about playing video games and watching too much television.

"Dream on," I told him. "Nothing *that* cool is ever going to happen in *this* town. You think I could maybe have one of those cookies before you finish the whole bag?"

Riley held the bag out to me so I could get *one* cookie. I took a bite. Riley rubbed the back of his neck and watched a bulldozer tear up a patch of earth. "Maybe they're building some kind of shopping mall."

"Yeah, right," I snorted. "With our luck, they're probably plowing everything under so they can plant a new kind of pine tree they've just invented."

McCreeville is not the kind of town where anything ever happens. When the big lumber mill closed down, and most of the town moved away, McCreeville more or less fell asleep. The city council keeps trying to think of ways to get new businesses to come to town, but no one in their right mind would want to move a business out here with the owls and the squirrels.

Everyone thought things would change last year when Mayor Pickett got elected and the new highway came through about a mile outside town, but, except for the odd car looking desperately for a gas station, the highway hasn't changed much of anything. The mayor keeps trying to attract tourists to our little town—he keeps talking about his big plans to put McCreeville on the tourist map—but there's nothing here anyone wants to see, unless they're *really* into trees.

3

Last fall, the town put up a big wooden sign out on the road that leads from the new highway to our town:

```
WELCOME TO MCCREEVILLE
```

I guess they thought it would make the town seem more friendly—more the kind of place a tired tourist might want to stop for the night. But it was only a matter of days before someone carved a new slogan into the sign with a pocketknife, so now it reads:

```
WELCOME TO MCCREEVILLE
    nothing but treeville
```

I watched the logging crew topple a tall pine and go at it with chain saws. At least now there would be fewer trees.

Riley grinned. "Maybe they're building some kind of top secret UFO base," he said with a gleam in his eye.

I laughed. Not many of us in town watch TV—you just can't get any channels way out here in the woods. But Riley's family has a big satellite dish that gets about a million-and-a-half channels, and Riley spends a lot of time watching dumb movies. Top secret UFO bases are right up his alley. "You really should try to spend more time in the real world," I told him. "You might actually start to like it."

A bulldozer roared by about a hundred feet behind our back fence, and for a few seconds it was too noisy to talk. The ground rumbled so much that the stones in Mom's rock garden began to click against each other. It was supposed to be a rose garden, and Mom had decorated it with stones from the river. But all the roses died, so now we just call it her rock garden.

"Maybe it's a hospital for the criminally insane," Riley shouted once the sound started to die away. "And one of the inmates is going to escape into the forest, where he'll train a pack of wild wolves. And together they'll hunt down the people who were responsible for putting him in the hospital."

I looked at Riley a long time. Sometimes it seems like he belongs on another planet. "There are no wolves in those woods," I reminded him. 'There aren't even bears anymore. All the interesting animals bailed out of here years ago. Your escaped inmate is going to have to train an army of squirrels."

"Squirrels will do," Riley said. "He'll just have to get a lot of 'em." He held the empty cookie bag over his open mouth and shook out the crumbs. Maybe Mom was right: too much TV *does* soften your brain.

I looked back out in the cleared part of the forest. It seemed odd to have so much sunlight in our back yard. "Maybe it's going to be a magazine distribution center," I told Riley.

"Huh?"

I grinned. "You can finally get a *Life*," I told him.

Riley groaned. "That was quite possibly the worst joke you've ever told," he said. He wadded up the empty bag and threw it at the trash cans lined up against the back fence. He missed by a mile.

A week later, the stumps were all gone from behind my house, and the ground was perfectly level. My back gate seemed to be the property line. If I stood in the back gate, all the land to my left was pine trees, brush, and grass. The land to the right was a vast field of loose brown dirt.

Riley came and knocked on my back door after school, like he usually does, and the two of us headed into the woods with my pellet gun and my

golden retriever, Sky. We cut across the newly leveled ground with Sky trotting between us. When I
looked behind us, I could see the trail of our footprints leading back to the gate. On the far side of
the clearing, workmen were putting up a high
fence. The noise of their hammers came to us
faintly across the flat dirt.

When we'd cut across the clearing, we found
our usual trail at the edge of the forest and headed
back to Hocket's Meadow, a little clearing in the
middle of the woods. All afternoon we shot at tin
cans with my pellet gun. Riley insisted that the cans
were some kind of radioactive cockroaches he'd
seen last night on a monster movie, and I just went
along with him. When we got bored with shooting,
we threw some pine cones for Sky to fetch.

Just then, a dark cloud passed over us, hiding
the sun, and I felt a sudden chill. The radio had
forecast rain tonight—where I live we get a *lot* of
rain—so Riley and I headed back through the
woods toward home. We came out of the forest just
about where we'd gone in.

The clearing looked like a wide, brown lake
between me and my house, with a couple of rusty
bulldozers floating on the surface. The air was
silent—the workers had all gone home. Off to the
right, in the late afternoon light, I could still see our

trail of footprints leading across the dirt from my back gate.

Riley and I started walking across the flat ground. It was soft and grainy under our sneakers, and the smell of dirt almost erased the smell of pine trees.

Riley picked up a dirt clod and threw it so that it exploded against the side of a bulldozer parked nearby. "Maybe they're going to build some kind of university," Riley said. "The Center for Advanced Studies in Boredom. This would be the perfect place."

I picked up my own dirt clod and threw it at the bulldozer, but it curved to the left and sailed too high. It landed far beyond its target. Sky took off running after it. I suppose he thought it was a pine cone. He raised a small cloud of brown dust behind him as he sprinted across the ground.

"You're not going to like the taste of that one," I yelled after him.

"That's one stupid dog," Riley said.

"Yeah," I agreed. "I think it's because he watches so much TV."

Sky bounded over to where the dirt clod had landed. He sniffed at the ground and wagged his tail. He started digging at the dirt with his front paws. He whined a little and then barked twice.

"What's he doing?" Riley asked me.

"It looks like he's found something," I said.

I called Sky's name, but he just looked up at me and then went back to pawing the ground. He'd obviously found something that piqued his interest. I called his name again. He didn't even look up this time.

"Come on," I said to Riley. "Let's go see what he's so interested in."

Riley and I plodded through the loose dirt to where Sky was tearing at the ground with his front paws. Riley grabbed Sky by the collar and pulled him back. I squatted down and dusted away the dirt with my fingertips. Imbedded in the loose soil was a dome-shaped white rock.

But it *wasn't* a rock. It had a weird, squiggly crack that ran down the middle, and when I rapped on it with my knuckle, it sounded hollow. I looked up at Riley. He had a puzzled look on his face. Sky whimpered and pulled at his collar.

The soil was very loose, so I had no trouble digging away the dirt around the object. In a couple of minutes, I'd dug it loose. I gave it a yank and it came free in my hands. As soon as I saw what it was, I dropped it to the dirt. It lay there grinning up at me, a huge, white skull—about the size of a volleyball.

I stood up. My knees felt weak. Sky barked at the skull.

"What is *that?*" Riley said. "A bear or something?"

I squatted back down. The skull was gleaming white, like someone had washed it. It had huge, uneven, yellowish teeth in its broad jaw. There was a ridge of bone over the eye sockets.

"I don't know," I said. "Maybe it's a gorilla or something."

"A gorilla?" Riley snorted. "Of course! The woods are full of them. You can't swing a banana around here without hitting a gorilla."

"OK," I said. "You tell me what it is."

Riley bent closer to the skull. "I have no idea," he admitted. "But it's no gorilla." I looked across the leveled dirt at the houses on the edge of town, including my own, and wondered what we should do.

"Maybe we should dig around here and see if there are some other bones," I suggested. I stared raking at the loose dirt with my fingers.

"Are you *kidding?*" Riley said. "Stop that! You're never supposed to disturb a crime scene. You've *already* got your fingerprints all over that dirt."

"Crime scene?" I said.

Riley just shook his head. "You don't have a clue, do you, Erich?" he said. "When someone finds a skeleton it always turns out to be a crime scene. Don't you ever watch TV?"

Sky pulled himself closer while Riley struggled to keep a grip on his collar. The dog kept pulling until he had edged close enough to sniff the skull. His hackles rose instantly. He whimpered, jerked himself free of Riley's grasp, and sprinted for home. I've never seen him so scared.

Riley stood up and watched Sky run. Neither of us made a move to stop him or call him back. We were both too stunned.

I looked back at the skull, which seemed to be staring up at me with its empty eye sockets. A cold wind blew across the field from the forest, kicking up small clouds of dust. "What do we do?" I asked Riley.

"Call someone, I guess."

"Who?"

Riley looked down at the skull and then ran his fingers back through his hair. "Let's call the cops," he said. "I've always wanted to dial 9–1–1."

As if agreeing with him, the skull rocked gently in the wind—nodding yes.

# Chapter 2

It was easy to lead Deputy Cassidy back to the skull. We followed the line of our own footsteps in the loose dirt. The sky was completely overcast now, and the sun had nearly gone down behind the tree line. It was pretty dark, but we could still make out the tracks.

Deputy Cassidy was a big-time deer hunter—he was practically a legend in these parts. I was hoping he'd take one look at the skull and tell us what it was. After all, he'd disassembled just about every kind of animal that lives in these parts.

When we got to the skull, Deputy Cassidy squatted down next to it and took off his hat. He scratched his head. He looked out toward the woods and then back down at the skull. "Don't that beat all?" he said. "I've never seen anything like it."

"You have any idea what it is?" Riley asked him.

Deputy Cassidy shook his head. "I haven't got a clue," he said. He pulled the long flashlight off his belt and shone its beam for a better look. The skull lit up an eerie white against the dark soil. "If I didn't know better, I'd say it was some sort of gorilla," the deputy said.

I gave Riley my I-told-you-so look. He just rolled his eyes.

Deputy Cassidy had me hold his flashlight, while he sifted through the dirt around where we'd dug out the skull. Before long, he uncovered a huge rib cage. I moved the flashlight closer to get a better look. Shadows of the bones seemed to crawl across the dirt when the light moved.

"Should you be doing this?" Riley asked, sounding a little anxious. "Isn't this disturbing a crime scene?" Deputy Cassidy stopped digging and looked at Riley, as though he wasn't sure if Riley was pulling his leg.

"*What?*" Riley said. "Am I the *only* one here who watches police shows?"

"I *am* the police," Deputy Cassidy pointed out. "I'm the one who's *supposed* to dig it up—and I could use a little help."

Riley blushed, but he took the hint. He got down on his knees in the dirt and worked silently alongside the deputy. They dug with their fingers and piled the dirt behind them while I held the flashlight. In a few minutes it was completely dark, and stars began to fill the sky.

Riley uncovered two long arm bones. At the end of the arm was a massive hand—the bones held perfectly in place by the surrounding soil. I shone the flashlight while Deputy Cassidy knelt and studied the huge hand. He pulled his nightstick from his belt and poked it at the long, white finger bones. I noticed I was holding my breath.

"This is the weirdest thing I've ever seen," Deputy Cassidy said. "It's not human, but it's not anything else, either."

It was pretty creepy out there in the cold and the dark, with nothing but a flashlight for light, and a big, weird skeleton half dug up. I was scared. I felt chills down my neck, and it wasn't just from the cold wind. I wished I was back in my bright, warm living room, reading a book.

Riley stood up and dusted off his knees. He held out one hand to me. His fingers were brown with dirt. "My turn to hold the flashlight," he told me. "You need to do some digging."

There was nothing I could do. I handed him the flashlight and got down on my knees. I paused a moment before plunging my hands into the loose dirt. I didn't mind *looking* at the skeleton; I just didn't want to *touch* it. I closed my eyes for a few seconds and offered up a prayer. Glenn, the youth leader at my church, once taught a lesson about the verse in Deuteronomy that says, "The Lord himself goes before you and will be with you; he will never leave you nor forsake you. Do not be afraid; do not be discouraged." I liked the verse so much I had gone home and memorized it. I repeated it in my mind now.

"Come on, Erich," Riley said, shining the flashlight in my eyes. "What are you waiting for? You afraid of ruining your manicure?"

I took a deep breath and slipped my fingers beneath the soil about four feet below the rib cage, hoping I'd miss the skeleton entirely. Instead, I immediately touched something sharp and hard. I felt the hair on the back of my neck stand on end, but I tried not to show Riley and the deputy how scared I was. I swallowed my fear and kept digging until a row of long, twisted, bony toes jutted up from the dirt.

A flash of lightning made me jump, and then thunder rumbled across the sky. I took a deep breath to regain my composure and then started digging again, faster than before. We wouldn't have much time before the rain came on.

I dug away at the loose earth until both feet were completely uncovered. They were huge—at least two feet long! A drop of rain plunked on the ground beside me, and then another and another. I stood up and looked at the whole skeleton; the skull and ribcage were very big—but even so, these feet seemed much too large for the rest of the body.

"I bet he had trouble finding shoes that fit," Riley said.

"Whatever it was, it didn't need shoes," Deputy Cassidy said. A second flash of lightning lit up his face. "I think we'd better stop right here and call this one in. Mayor Pickett's going to want to hear about this."

"See," Riley told me, shining the flashlight at his own face so I could see him in the dark. "It's a crime scene." He made a face at me. It was drizzling now.

"It's *no* crime scene," Deputy Cassidy said, flipping up the collar of his jacket. "I'm sure of that."

I looked down at the skeleton. It flickered brightly in another flash of lightning. The big yellow teeth grinned up at us, glistening in the rain.

"It's no crime scene," Deputy Cassidy said again. "But that's the *only* thing I'm sure of."

We followed him through the mud to the safety of my warm, dry house. I thanked the Lord each step of the way.

# Chapter 3

The next morning, I woke up half an hour before my alarm went off. I sat up in bed, still a bit groggy, and looked at the window. The storm had passed. Dawn was just breaking, but I could hear voices and cars down behind my house. A beam of light lit up my curtains, and a dim shadow crawled across the ceiling and down the wall. It was far too early for the workmen to be out there working.

I got up and went to the window. Pulling back the curtain, I looked outside. All kinds of trucks and vans were parked down in the cleared part of the forest—right where we'd found the skeleton last night. The vehicles created a ring of bright light in the middle of the dark field. Some of the trucks had big satellite dishes on them. Cables ran everywhere in the muddy dirt.

Most of the trucks and vans had logos or letters on their sides: KWRB, Eyewitness News, Current Edition. There were more than a dozen television cameras down there. I noticed that one of them was pointed in the direction of our house. I stepped back from the window and let the curtain fall across the window again. What were they all doing down there?

I sat down on my bed. There probably hadn't been an actual television camera in McCreeville since television was invented—and now there were a ton of them practically in my backyard. What was going on here?

I knew I'd have to call Riley. He watched more television than anyone I knew. He was the town's foremost expert. If anyone knew what was going on, it would be Riley.

I wanted to go downstairs to the kitchen phone and give him a call, but it was much too early. Everyone would be asleep at his house. I sat down on my bed, rubbed my eyes, and tried to think clearly. By the time it was late enough to call Riley's house, all the commotion behind my house might be over. If I wanted to know what was going on, I'd have to go down there myself.

I put on my clothes and yanked a big sweater over my head. I pulled on my tennis shoes and tied the laces. I crept downstairs as quietly as I could so as not to wake anyone.

When I pushed open the back door, the damp air and the smell of pines hit me like a wet towel. I stole across the dewy back yard, past Mom's rock garden, and slipped through the back gate without waking Sky. I latched the gate shut behind me.

I stopped at the edge of the grass, where the bulldozers had left the ground untouched, and looked across the wide field of mud at the cluster of television trucks. Did I really want to stomp across all that mud just to see what was going on? I looked down at my bright white tennis shoes. *Oh well,* I thought. *When will there ever be a news truck in McCreeville again?* I stepped into the mud and made my way slowly over to the bright lights and commotion.

When I neared the vans, I tried to pay close attention so that I could describe everything to Riley when I saw him. I studied all the equipment—the tangled cables running everywhere, the satellite dishes, the bright lights and cameras—and tried to memorize each detail.

A cameraman knelt in the mud, aiming his camera at the skeleton, which someone had dug around with a shovel. Orange pylons surrounded the scene now, and a blue tarp lay crumpled in the mud. I figured it had been used to protect the bones from last night's rain. Another cameraman aimed his camera across the field toward the pine forest, now lit with the first soft rays of sunlight.

As I passed a gap between two of the vans, I glimpsed a third cameraman filming an interview. A man wearing a headset and holding a clipboard stood next to the cameraman. He held up five fingers and then counted down to one. A woman in a suit, who didn't look happy to be standing ankle deep in mud, began talking into a microphone, and then held the microphone out to Riley.

*Riley?*

I stopped dead in my muddy tracks. I took a step back so I could see between the vans and saw Riley blinking in the bright light. He grinned like an idiot and talked into the microphone held by the woman in the suit.

I slipped over and stood next to the cameraman. The man with the clipboard grabbed me firmly by the shoulder and put a finger up to his lips. He bent close to my ear. "Quiet," he whispered. "This is a live feed. Don't make any noise."

I nodded.

"We have here a young boy named Sigfried Grump," the woman said. I glanced around, wondering who she was talking about.

"And how did you make this incredible discovery, Sigfried?" the woman said into the microphone. She tilted the microphone toward a dopey-looking Riley Hope.

Riley gathered himself up importantly. I'm sure he'd been waiting his whole life to be on television, and he seemed to be enjoying the moment.

He looked the woman in the eye. "I've always been fascinated by forensic paleontology," he said gravely. "I guess you could say that archaeology and anthropology run in my veins. So when the opportunity to explore this site presented itself . . ." Riley turned to look at the camera, with one eyebrow raised, and saw me standing there with my arms crossed.

Riley stopped in mid-sentence. His eyebrow settled back into place and his mouth fell open a little. He glanced over at the woman interviewing him and back at me. "Actually, my friend's dog dug it up," he said abruptly and took off running.

Everyone stood still for a second, stunned. Then the man with the clipboard frantically drew his finger across his throat, but the woman in the suit wasn't paying attention. She was watching Riley sprint across the mud toward my house. I could hear Riley laughing.

The man with the clipboard looked down at me. He didn't look pleased. He seemed to think I had something to do with all this, so I took off running too. I didn't know what else to do.

When I caught up to Riley, he was hiding behind the trash cans outside my back fence. We keep them there so Sky won't knock them over at night looking for scraps.

I was breathless and spattered with mud. I crouched down beside Riley. He was laughing so hard he could barely breathe. "Come on," I said. We ducked past Dad's woodpile and through the gate into my back yard. We crouched down behind the fence so we'd be hidden.

"*Sigfried Grump?*" I said. "What was *that* all about?"

"Keep your voice down," Riley hissed. "They might be looking for us." Riley leaned against the fence. "I saw them on the news this morning," he whispered. "I headed over here so I could be on television—but you had to come along and mess everything up."

"You saw them on the news?" I said.

"Practically every news agency in the state showed up," Riley said laughing. "Everyone but Mr. Nestor." Mr. Nestor was the editor of the McCreeville *Weekly Sentinel*, the town's newspaper.

"The biggest news story in town history, and our own newspaper slept right through it!"

"You mean it actually turned out to be a crime scene?"

"Nah," Riley whispered. "It's even better. You'll never guess what they're saying."

"What?" I asked. "What are they saying?"

"The skeleton we dug up definitely isn't human," Riley said. "But nobody knows what it is." He leaned closer to me and lowered his voice even more—although there was clearly no one around to hear. "They think it might be a Sasquatch."

"*What* kind of squash?"

"Not a squash, you dweeb," Riley whispered. "A *Sasquatch*. You know, like Bigfoot."

"*What!?*"

"*Shhhhhh.*"

Sky barked suddenly. I guess I woke him up when I yelled. He peeked out of his doghouse and barked again. When he saw who it was, he came trotting over with his tail wagging.

"Remember the huge feet?" Riley said. "Remember how Deputy Cassidy said he'd never seen a skeleton like it? Well, that's why. It's a Sasquatch."

I looked at him a long time without saying anything. It was hard to know if he was pulling my leg.

I straightened up. I stood on my tiptoes and peeked over the fence at the news vans.

Riley stood next to me. He didn't have to stand on his tiptoes to see over. A Bigfoot. It all seemed a little far-fetched to me.

Sky nuzzled at my hand, so I scratched him behind the ears as I peered over the fence. "I don't know," I told Riley. "There's got to be a scientific explanation."

"*Scientific?!*" Riley sputtered. "This *is* science. You'd know about these things if you watched more television. Both *Search for Sasquatch* and *Bigfoot Encounters* were on just last week." Riley's eyes were wide with excitement. It was clear he really thought Bigfoot was a possibility. He was that kind of guy.

"My mom always said that watching too much TV could soften your brain," I told him. "But until this moment, I didn't believe her."

"That skeleton wasn't *on television,*" Riley reminded me. "It was practically in your back yard. You saw it yourself."

He had a point, but the whole idea of Bigfoot seemed absurd. "There's no such thing as Bigfoot," I told him. "It's a myth."

Riley looked at me seriously. "Don't be so skeptical," he advised me. "It's dangerous."

*"Dangerous?"*

"Yeah," Riley said. "The skeptics are always the ones who get eaten in Bigfoot movies."

As if he understood what we were saying, Sky whimpered and trotted back to the safety of his doghouse.

While we were at school that day, they dug up the whole skeleton and packed it off somewhere. They said it was going to be studied by scientists. Everyone at school was talking about it, but no one believed it was really the remains of Bigfoot. They all seemed to think it was some kind of prank that Riley and I had cooked up.

Personally, I didn't know what to think. The whole Bigfoot idea seemed pretty silly. But there was something about it that I couldn't get out of my mind. For the next few days, the image of the skeleton—lit up in a flash of lightning—kept interrupting my thoughts. I'd be sitting at my desk in history class, and suddenly I'd imagine what that huge set of bones would look like covered with muscles and fur. None of the pictures I invented looked very friendly.

Every night, the huge gorilla-like monster haunted my dreams. Each morning, I woke up more tired than when I'd gone to bed, and found the sheets twisted around my body from all my tossing and turning.

I was tempted to go to the library to see if they had any books about Bigfoot, but the idea was too silly. Even if someone *had* written a book about it, that didn't mean that Bigfoot existed. There were books about UFOs and the Loch Ness Monster and all kinds of crazy things.

What I knew I really should do was ask my dad. He taught science at McCreeville High. He was always reading, and he'd lived in this town all his life. He'd know what was going on. But it was hard to bring up such a lame question.

All week I kept wondering what would happen if there were *more* Bigfoots—or would it be *Bigfeet?*—still living out in the woods behind my house.

I tried to convince myself that it was impossible—but the more I thought about it, the less convinced I was. I knew the forest stretched for hundreds of square miles—it was a huge green patch all around our town on the map. Who knew *what* might be living out there?

I usually took Sky for a walk in the woods every day after school. I liked to unclip his leash and let him run. But all that week I hooked the leash to his collar and took him into the middle of town instead. There was something about all the buildings and people that relaxed me. I felt like a sissy, but digging up a giant skeleton can make you a little nervous.

I was walking Sky past all the parked cars on Main Street one day when I heard someone call my name. I looked across the street. Mr. Nestor, the editor of the McCreeville *Weekly Sentinel*, stood in the doorway of the newspaper office waving for me to come over. I looked both ways and then tugged on Sky's leash. We crossed the street.

I thought he must want to ask me about the skeleton—everyone in town was talking about it— but that's not what he wanted. "Are you in the big Teen Shuffleboard Tournament next week?" he asked. I wasn't exaggerating when I said that shuffleboard was the hottest activity for the kids in our town!

"Me?" I said, a little surprised. "No. I don't really play much shuffleboard."

"Too bad," Mr. Nestor said. "I need to interview someone who plays for a big story I'm working on." Mr. Nestor looked down at Sky.

"He doesn't play either," I told him. I meant it to be a joke, but Mr. Nestor just nodded wistfully. "What's the big story about?" I asked him.

"Oh, the town shuffleboard deck was struck by lightning in last week's storm," Mr. Nestor said. "Part of it got destroyed, and the big tournament is only a few days away."

Like I said: this is a pretty boring town.

"Sorry I can't help you," I told Mr. Nestor. Sky and I left him standing in the doorway scanning the street for another teenager.

Oddly, bumping into Mr. Nestor relaxed me a lot. Just knowing that this was a town where a story on a damaged shuffleboard deck could make the front page made it seem unlikely that we'd ever be visited by a Sasquatch!


I sat at my desk that afternoon, trying to do homework, but I kept getting distracted. The workmen and all the machinery behind the house made quite a racket, and it was hard to concentrate. I got up and went to the window and looked out at the tall fence that now surrounded the construction site. What was going on in there?

I looked along the line of trees at the edge of the woods. I pressed my forehead against the cool glass and tried to see all the way to Bear Mountain through the mist. There had to be hundreds of thousands of pine trees out there covering hundreds of thousands of acres. How hard would it be for a whole tribe of Bigfeet (I had decided that *Bigfeet* was the proper term) to hide there? How much did we *really* know about what lived in those woods? I thought of the huge skull grinning up at me from the ground.

"Erich," a voice said behind me. I just about jumped out of my skin. I spun around.

My mom stood in the doorway, giving me an odd look. "Are you OK, Erich?" she asked.

"Yeah," I told her, forcing a smile. "Really. Wonderful. I'm great. Absolutely."

Mom just looked at me a few seconds. "Dinner's ready," she told me.

"Has anyone said anything about the bones you found last week?" Dad asked from across the dinner table when we finished saying grace. "You never told me what happened."

I had the feeling that Dad already knew everything and was just trying to get me to talk about it. I glanced over at Mom. Had she told him about the way I'd jumped when she came up behind me?

"They said some nonsense about Bigfoot," I told Dad. "Some scientist took the bones away to study them. He said this might finally be proof that Bigfoot exists."

"Why do you think the news would broadcast something as silly as that?" Dad asked. He took a sip of water.

It seemed like Dad was trying to lead me to something. Like I said, he's the science teacher at McCreeville High, and I know he likes to teach his students mostly by asking them questions.

I thought about his question a moment, and then I suddenly knew the answer. "They're just trying to improve their ratings," I said. "They're trying to get people to watch their show."

Dad nodded. I knew I'd given him the answer he'd expected. He stabbed a piece of meat loaf with his fork. "Well, what about this *scientist?*" Dad asked, giving special stress to the word *scientist.* "*That* sounds very important."

I was right with him. "You can find scientists who will say just about anything," I told him. "Just because you call yourself a scientist doesn't mean you aren't a nut."

Dad smiled and nodded again. He had a way of making me see things clearly. I popped some meat loaf into my mouth and chewed. It was all beginning to make sense. It was like a weight was lifted from my shoulders.

"What do you think those bones were *really* from?" I asked Dad. "How do *you* explain the skeleton?"

"I can't explain it," Dad admitted. "But I can't explain why gravity works either. I just know there's no such thing as Bigfoot." He dabbed at his mouth with his napkin. "I've lived in this town my whole life, and I've spent more time in these woods than just about anyone. Trust me: there are no monsters out there."

There was something about Dad's voice that soothed me. It was true when I was a little kid, and it was still true now. I knew there was nothing to be scared of. I smiled across the table at him. I was cured. I had no worries. Bigfoot was the last thing on my mind after that.

Until one night the next week . . .

# Chapter 4

I sat bolt upright in bed. My heart pounded. I glanced over at my alarm clock. It was just after two in the morning. I tried to remember if I'd been having a dream, but I couldn't recall a thing. I had no idea what woke me up. Maybe something was going on in the construction site. I lay back on my pillow and tried to calm myself down.

Then I heard it.

There was a loud moaning and the sound of trash cans being knocked around. Sky was barking crazily, and I could hear him scratching at the doggie door, like he does when he wants to be let in.

The raccoons were in the trash cans again. It happened every spring. I groaned. I knew I was the one who would have to clean up the mess. Sky whined loudly and scratched at the door again.

Usually he loved chasing raccoons, and he'd be digging around the back fence trying to get out at them—but these last couple of weeks had changed him. He was spooked easily, and he wanted to spend all his time inside the house.

There was more clanging of trash cans and more loud whining. I went to the window and pulled it open. "Shhhh," I called softly down to Sky. "You're going to wake everyone up." I shivered in the cold night air that seeped in through the window. Usually at the sound of my voice, Sky stopped barking, but this time he just started whining and yelping louder. He tore at the back door with his claws.

I groaned and rubbed my eyes. I didn't want to go out in the cold, but if I could shoo away the raccoons, I'd have a whole lot less work to do in the morning. And maybe Sky and I could both get some sleep.

I pulled on the same clothes I'd worn yesterday. I tied up my shoes and slipped into my jacket. I slowly creaked open my door and crept downstairs. Turning on the kitchen light, I tiptoed to the back door. I peered through the window in the top half of the door, but the kitchen light was too bright— all I could see was my own reflection.

When I pulled the door open, Sky pushed past me and sprinted through the kitchen, his claws scrabbling across the tile floor. He disappeared into the living room. I called to him, but he wouldn't come back. I just shook my head. I'd have to find him and take him outside when I was done moving the trash cans.

The yard looked damp and misty. I could barely see the back fence in the rectangle of light that shone through the doorway. The full moon was a faint yellow glow high in the sky. There was too much fog to see stars. I gathered my jacket more tightly around me and crept down the back steps.

Raccoons are weird animals. They can be hard to scare away once they get used to being around people, and they can be very destructive when they want to be. To tell you the truth, those little masks give me the creeps. I wasn't sure how I would shoo them away. As I walked slowly across the yard toward the back fence, I tried to think of a plan—a way to scare them away without having to get too close to them.

I got an idea. I stooped down and ran my hand over the damp ground where Mom had her rock garden. I found a couple of good sized round stones. I thought I'd lob a couple of them over the fence and give the raccoons a good scare. I pictured them diving off the trash can and scattering in every direction. I grinned. This would be kind of fun.

I tiptoed over to the fence and crouched down. On the other side I could hear a lot of commotion. It sounded like there might be a dozen of the pesky little things. I weighed the two stones in my hands. I decided on the bigger of the two. I pressed myself against the fence and pretended the stone was a hand grenade. I raised it to my teeth, pulled out the imaginary pin, and lobbed the grenade sidearm, high over the fence.

I heard a furry thud, and a deep, angry groan on the other side of the fence. The groan was much too deep to be a raccoon. The hair on the back of my neck suddenly stood on end. I crouched there frozen. Something felt terribly wrong.

There was a long moment of silence. I glanced up just in time to see a trash can rocket high into the air from the other side of the fence. It seemed to hang high in the sky a moment—at least twenty feet off the ground—completely blotting out the moon. Then it crashed to the ground a few feet from where I was hiding. Trash exploded everywhere.

I didn't know what to do. I wanted to run, but for some reason I couldn't move. I just crouched there, leaning against the damp fence, holding my breath. I strained to hear what was happening on the other side of the fence.

And then a sound sent chills down my back.

It was a deep, angry, resonant growl—so loud it seemed to fill the yard and vibrate in my bones. My knees shook beneath me. I had never been so terrified.

Whatever I'd hit with the rock definitely *wasn't* a raccoon. And it sure wasn't happy with me either. I took off running toward the house, stumbling over rocks and potted plants. Another trash can thudded to the ground behind me, but I didn't dare look back. I kept my eyes fixed on the open back door.

I bounded up the back steps and slammed the door behind me. I twisted the lock. I dashed through the kitchen and scrambled up the stairs. It never occurred to me to knock on my parents' door; I just sprinted down the hall to my own bedroom.

When I stumbled into my room, I still had the second stone in my hand. I looked down it at. It was gray and heavy, about the size of a baseball. It was a natural weapon—but it was no match for whatever had launched those trash cans into the air!

I set the stone on my desk and crept to the window. I peeked out. On the far side of the fence, trash was strewn everywhere, but whatever had been there was gone.

The moon hung large and pale over the misty forest. Everything was silent. I went over and sat on my bed.

I tried to remember the talk I'd had with my dad at the dinner table. Dad was the smartest person I knew. He was a *science* teacher. He'd lived in these woods all his life. If he said there was no Bigfoot, there was no Bigfoot. Period. End of story. There had to be another explanation for what just happened to me.

"There's no such thing as Bigfoot," I whispered to myself, sitting there on the bed. "It simply doesn't exist."

I said it, but I didn't sound nearly as convincing as my dad.

# Chapter 5

I didn't get much sleep the rest of the night, and when the sun came up I was lying in bed, wide awake, staring up at the ceiling. I went to the window and looked down at the scene behind my house. Trash was scattered all over the back yard, and the patch of grass behind our house was all torn up and muddy. It looked like a stampede of elephants had come through during the night.

I knew I'd have to pick up all the trash, but if I did it before Mom and Dad got up, I wouldn't have to explain how it happened. They wouldn't believe it if I told them. I wasn't sure I believed it myself.

I put on my clothes and crept downstairs, and before Mom and Dad's radio alarm clock sounded, the backyard was cleaned up and the trash cans were lined up neatly against the back fence as though nothing had happened. Two of the trash cans had large dents in them, but I positioned them so that the dents were facing the fence. I hoped no one would notice.

"So you're saying that there's some kind of Bigfoot living behind your house?" Riley asked. We were sitting in the crowded cafeteria at lunch that day, and I'd made the mistake of telling Riley everything.

"Could you *please* keep your voice down?" I begged him. "That's not what I said at all. I didn't say anything about Bigfoot."

"Well, what else could it be?" Riley bellowed. "Of *course* it's a Bigfoot." I could feel everyone's eyes on us. I glanced around. Everyone at the tables around us suddenly looked down at their food, like they were concentrating on eating. No one was talking. I knew all of them were listening to us—but they didn't want to look like they were.

"There's no such thing as Bigfoot," I said loudly, hoping everyone listening would think Riley was the only crazy one. "Bigfoot is a myth."

"Dude," Riley said. "We dug up a Bigfoot skeleton a couple of weeks ago. And now you've got some kind of monster launching trash cans into orbit. What else could it be? A whole tribe of Bigfoots probably lives back there."

"Big*feet*," I corrected him, leaning across the table. "And not so loud."

"OK. *Bigfeet*. Whatever," Riley said, even louder. His eyes were wide. He was letting himself get carried away. "Anyway, I'll bet a whole tribe of them lived in that patch of woods, and now the town cut them down and they're all ticked."

I heard some muffled laughter, but when I glanced around, everyone was still quietly looking down at their food, trying not to smile. "Riley," I begged him. "Could you just be quiet for a moment? Could we maybe continue this discussion later?"

Riley ignored me. "If this is anything like *Dark Night on Bigfoot Mountain*—which I saw on TV just last Tuesday night—it's only a matter of time before they get organized and attack the town," Riley said.

Now the laughter wasn't even muffled. I was too embarrassed to look around. "Riley Hope, could you just shut up a minute?" I said. "This isn't some dumb movie. There's no such thing as Bigfoot. You've spent so much time in front of your television you can't function in the real world anymore."

"Can't function?" Riley sputtered. "I'm the only person in this stupid town who'll know what to do when we finally get attacked. I've been preparing my whole life for this."

There was a loud snicker and then some uncontrollable coughing and snorting behind me. I think someone spat milk through their nose, but I didn't turn to look—I was too embarrassed. I could feel every eye in the cafeteria on me now. I slouched down in my chair, wishing I could turn invisible.

"Wait till the Bigfeet come marching through town armed with clubs," Riley bellowed. "We'll see who can function in the real world."

That afternoon, Riley came around and knocked on my back door. He wanted to go out in the woods; even though it was cloudy, and I had heard on the radio that there was a sixty percent chance of rain by nightfall. Of course I didn't want to go, but I couldn't come up with much of an excuse. After all, *I* was the one who kept saying I didn't believe in Bigfoot. I made sure we took along my pellet gun—so we could shoot at cans, of course.

As we walked along beside the construction site fence in the warm light of day, things didn't seem as scary. It was just the same ole' woods I'd grown up in—nothing to be nervous about. Even Sky trotted along beside me, his bushy tail wagging serenely in the air. We got to the end of the fence and headed in among the trees, leaving the sounds of machinery and workmen behind.

Instead of worrying about monsters, I started to worry about the other kids at school. "You need to learn when to keep your mouth shut," I told Riley as we walked. "You made us look pretty crazy at lunch today. Not everyone understands your sense of humor."

*"Sense of humor?"* Riley sputtered. "I was totally and completely serious."

"You *were not,*" I told him. "And now everyone at school is calling us the Bigfoot Brothers. We'll never live it down."

Riley stopped walking and turned to look at me. *He* seemed to be getting ticked at *me,* which didn't make a lot of sense. He held his hand up in front of my face, pointing one finger at the sky. "Number one: we dig up some huge skeleton in the clearing," Riley announced. He raised a second finger. "Number two: it has feet the size of my mom's station wagon. Number three: some big old monster ends up in your back yard throwing trash cans in the middle of the night. You do the math."

I had no idea how to explain any of the things he'd mentioned, but I just shook my head. "There's no such thing as Bigfoot," I said stubbornly. "Just ask my dad. He teaches science."

Riley just rolled his eyes.

When we got to Hockett's Meadow, Sky seemed to get a little nervous again, so I clipped his leash to his collar to keep him from bolting. I didn't want to let on, but seeing him so skittish made me a little nervous too.

"See that?" Riley said. "You know why your dog is spooked, don't you? He smells one of them." Riley looked around us at the thick trees. "It could be out there anywhere," he said dramatically. "It could be watching us right now."

I felt a shiver go through me, but I tried hard to look like I wasn't the least bit scared. "He probably just smells a squirrel," I said. "You know how he hates squirrels."

Riley peered at the trees like he was trying to see through them. "It was just like this in *Cold Night on Bigfoot Mountain*," he said. "It started out with these two guys and a dog, and they were hiking deep in the woods."

"I don't want to hear about your stupid movies," I said. "I just want to shoot at some cans."

Riley ignored me. "It was starting to get dark," he said slowly, trying to set the scene. "They were setting up their tent in a clearing—just like this one—when their dog started barking at something." Riley looked around at the thick woods. I wished he would stop talking. "But they couldn't see what was out there, because the trees were too thick."

As if on cue, Sky started to growl. I glanced down at him. He was looking out at the woods and pulling at his leash. He raised his hackles. I wrapped the leash around my hand a couple of times so I could hold him back if I had to.

"Then they heard a twig crack somewhere deep in the woods," Riley said slowly. "They had a rifle with them, and one of them picked it up and checked to be sure it was loaded."

I felt my hand tighten around the plastic stock of my pellet gun.

"They knew something was out there watching them from the woods," Riley went on looking around us at the trees. "But it was getting dark, and there was nothing they could do."

As if it was part of the script, the woods seemed to suddenly turn a few shades darker, like a cloud had just passed in front of the sun. To tell you the truth, Riley was giving me the heebie-jeebies. I didn't want to hear about the stupid movie; I just wanted to go home.

"As darkness began to fill the woods," Riley said, "they heard a strange breathing coming from all around them in the darkness. Minute by minute, the noise kept getting louder and closer—and the last thing they heard was . . ."

Just then, Sky barked angrily at the trees. I just about screamed. I gave the leash an angry jerk. "No!" I said. "Be quiet."

Riley smiled at me. "He can't help barking," he said. "He's a dog."

"I wasn't *talking* to the dog," I told him.

Riley took a step back and looked at me. He grinned. "You were scared," he said. "The story I was telling you was giving you the creeps."

"It *was* not," I told him.

"You thought we were about to get attacked by a bunch of monsters with oversized feet." Riley started laughing.

"I did not," I said angrily. "I thought I was going to get bored to death by some moron who watches too much TV." I pulled Sky closer to me.

Riley shook his head. He wasn't laughing now. "Admit it," he said. "At least for a minute, you thought there might be such a thing as a Sasquatch out here in these woods."

"Not a chance," I told him. "You're the only one in this town who's lame enough to believe in Bigfoot."

"Yeah?" he said. "Let's see who believes. You can just walk home on your own." He took off out of the clearing and headed back toward the house. In a few seconds, he was out of sight, but I could hear his footsteps crunching through the dry pine needles. I was all alone in the clearing, and it was getting dark and windy with the storm coming on.

Riley was right. I *was* spooked. I didn't want to be alone—but I couldn't very well go running after him after everything I'd said. I looked around at the darkening woods. I was getting goosebumps all over. I cocked the pellet gun and held it down at my side.

I didn't want to look like an idiot, so I waited in the clearing until I could barely hear Riley's footsteps up ahead, and then I pulled on Sky's leash, and we headed back through the woods after Riley.

As I walked among the trees, with Sky all skittish and nervous beside me, I had the weird feeling that someone was watching me from the shadows. It took all the self-control I had not to take off running after Riley.

The thing about being in the woods is that it gets dark long before the sun goes down—especially on a cloudy day like this. But as you get close to the edge of the woods, it almost seems like the sun is coming up, because it keeps getting brighter and brighter with each step you take.

I guess I was walking pretty fast, because by the time I got near the edge of the woods, I could see Riley up ahead in the scattered sunlight that filtered through the clouds and the tall trees. Just seeing him made me feel a little braver. I pulled back on Sky's leash and slowed my pace.

When Riley got to the edge of the woods, he suddenly stopped dead in his tracks in front of the white construction site fence. He looked down at something on the ground. He just stood there as I came up behind him. The construction site was silent now. Everyone had gone home for the day.

I was still a bit angry at Riley, but I walked over silently and stood next to him. I looked down at the ground in front of us.

*There it was*—a giant footprint in the mud at the edge of the forest. It was at least three feet long and maybe a foot wide. Except for the size, it looked human—with five twisted toes, a deep heel and a curved arch. I felt a shiver go through me again.

Sky sniffed around the edges of the footprint. His hackles immediately stood on end and he gave a deep growl.

Neither Riley nor I said anything. We just stood there looking down at the imprint in the mud. A cold breeze sent a chill down my spine.

"I didn't notice this when we were heading into the woods," I said. "Did you?"

"Don't you think a footprint the size of a Winnebago is the kind of thing I would have mentioned?" Riley said.

It *was* a pretty stupid question, but I wasn't thinking too clearly right then. "Maybe we went into the woods over there," I said, pointing farther along the high fence. "Maybe we just missed it."

"Yeah," Riley said. "Or maybe it just wasn't *here* yet when we went in."

The thought made my blood run cold. What if the thing that made this footprint was still nearby? I got a weird tingly feeling down the back of my neck. I glanced over my shoulder, just to make sure nothing was watching us from the dark woods. Of course, I couldn't see beyond the first few trees. *Anything* could be in there looking out at us.

Thunder rumbled over the treetops, and a soft rain began to fall. As the rain grew harder, it began to fill the big footprint with water. The muddy edges began to crumble. In a few minutes, the footprint would be gone. We wouldn't have a chance to show it to anyone else or to take a photograph. No one would ever believe us.

# Chapter 6

"L ook, boys," Mayor Pickett told us the next morning. "There's a logical explanation for all of this." He leaned back in his big leather chair and smiled. He put his hands, palm down, on his polished wooden desk. "There's nothing here to get excited about. You'll just have to take my word for it."

Mr. Pickett was mayor of McCreeville, but our town was so small that being mayor was only a part-time job. The rest of the time, he was an accountant at the town's last remaining lumber mill. It was Saturday morning, so the mayor was wearing jeans and a sweater instead of his usual suit and tie.

"But the footprint was bigger than this desk," Riley exaggerated. He was sitting on the edge of his chair, leaning across the mayor's desk. "And it threw a trash can a hundred feet in the air. It got into Erich's trash again last night. Don't you see? It's losing its fear of humans."

Mayor Pickett just smiled and shook his head. "There's nothing to worry about, boys," he said. "Let's not overreact."

"*Overreact!?*" Riley sputtered. "There's probably a whole tribe of angry Bigfoots—"

"Big*feet*," I corrected him.

Riley glared at me. "What*ever*," he said. "Bigfeet. Anyway, there's a whole bunch of 'em. And as the leading expert on monsters in this town, I'm telling you we're in serious trouble."

The mayor rocked back in his chair and put his feet on the desk. He linked his hands behind his neck so that his elbows stuck out on either side of his head. He smiled at Riley. "Riley Hope," he said. "You *say* you saw a giant footprint—but aren't you the same Riley Hope who reported a UFO last year when the Goodyear Blimp flew over?"

I looked over at Riley. This was news to me. "You *did*, Riles?"

Riley shrugged. "It was an honest mistake," he said. "It looked just like the mother ship on *Invasion from Planet X.*"

I groaned and shook my head. Another dumb movie!

"You dialed 9–1–1," Mayor Pickett went on. "You said we were being invaded by aliens. Deputy Cassidy and the whole Volunteer Fire Department went into action, and you gave Doris the dispatcher quite a shock."

I looked over at Riley again. "You told me you'd never called 9–1–1 before," I said.

Riley shrugged. "Do *you* remember every phone call *you* ever made?" he asked me.

My best friend wasn't playing with a full deck. Here was the proof. He was a nut, a lunatic, a complete wacko. And here *I* was, in the mayor's office, making a Bigfoot report with him. I felt like banging my head on the desk, but instead I ran my hand slowly down my face.

The mayor slipped his feet off the desk and leaned forward. He looked at Riley and then at me. He had a smile in his eyes. It was like he was remembering way back when he was a thirteen-year-old spaz like us. "Boys," he said. "You'll have to trust me on this one. There are *no* monsters living in the woods." He stood up and tugged down the hem of his sweater. "Now, I have a lot of work to do this morning. We have a major construction project in the works, so if you two will excuse me . . ."

Back out on the bright street, I walked silently beside Riley, feeling like an idiot. We passed the library, the post office, and the video store.

"This is exactly like in *Scream City*," Riley said at last.

"*What!?*" I said. He was talking about another movie! I thought my head was going to explode.

"In *Scream City* the mayor didn't want the police chief to tell anyone about the giant, mutant praying mantis," Riley explained. "He was afraid it would start a panic and ruin the tourist season."

This was more than I could take. I stopped walking and put my hands on the sides of my head. Riley turned to face me. "We don't *have* a tourist season!" I shouted. "We haven't had a tourist in McCreeville since I was born! All those stupid movies you watch have turned your brain to mush. You wouldn't recognize reality if it came up and bit you on the nose."

"OK, it's not *exactly* like *Scream City*," Riley conceded.

"We don't even have a *motel*," I went on. I was really worked up. "The only guy who ever stayed here overnight was that guy whose car broke down out on the highway—and *he* slept at *my* house."

"Easy. Easy," Riley said, trying to calm me down. "You're missing the point."

"And what *is* the point, Riley?" I shouted.

"The point is that, when it comes to monsters, mayors *always* make things worse," he said. "Think of it: *Night of the Giant Squid, Atomic Mutant III, Vampire Zombies from Mars*—the list goes on and on."

"Riley," I said. "Listen to me: There are *no* Martian zombies, there are *no* atomic mutants, there are *no* giant squids—OK maybe there *are* giant squids," I admitted. "But there are *no* Bigfoots."

"Big*feet*," Riley corrected me.

I was so hopping mad, I think I did an involuntary dance right there on the sidewalk. Riley backed away a few steps. "Leave me *alone*," I shouted. "Get out of my face. Get out of my life. Get out of my zip code."

"Dude, relax," Riley said. "You're going to rupture something."

"I'm sorry," I said. "You're driving me crazy. I don't want to play with you anymore. I have better things to do with my Saturday mornings."

"Erich, give me one more chance," Riley said. "You say Bigfoot doesn't exist, and I say he does. Let's settle it. I'll come over to your place tonight and we'll have an all-night Bigfoot vigil."

"A what?"

"Just tell your parents we're having a sleepover," Riley said. "We'll stay up all night. We'll keep a lookout. If Bigfoot doesn't show up to root through your garbage, I'll never say another word about it."

I sighed. It was probably the most sensible offer I'd ever get out of Riley Hope. I took a deep breath and tried to regain my composure. "OK," I said. "Sure. An all-night Bigfoot vigil."

Riley smiled cautiously. "One more thing," he said, placing his hands on my shoulders. It was clear he didn't want to get me upset again. "Can I come for dinner? Your mom's a better cook than mine."

I was in the living room, reading, when Riley knocked. When I got to the kitchen, I saw him through the window in the back door. I could smell the chicken Mom was baking for dinner. It occurred to me that we'd never had Riley over for dinner before. The sky outside was getting dark and cloudy again. He kicked at the door again, even though he could see me coming. He was balancing a stack of videos against his chest. I pulled open the door.

"About time," he said. "It's going to start raining any minute." He pushed past me into the kitchen. "Ummm," he said, sniffing the air and looking around. "I'm starved. This smells much better than what we ate at my house."

"You already ate dinner?" I asked him.

"Just one," he said. "I'm ready for another."

I glanced out the door before I closed it to make sure Riley had latched the gate behind him—just so Sky can't get out of the yard, I told myself. I led Riley into the living room.

"You already put the trash cans out back," Riley said. "So I guess everything is ready for our vigil." He set the stack of videos on the coffee table.

"What are all these for?" I asked him, tilting my head to read the titles.

"Research," he told me. "I rented every monster movie in town. We need to know what to expect."

I groaned. I was nervous enough about our all-night monster vigil without watching a bunch of scary movies. "I don't know if this is such a good idea," I told him.

"Relax," Riley said. "Think of it as a slumber party. We'll make popcorn. We'll do each other's hair. Maybe we'll see a monster. When's your mom serve dinner?"

When we all sat down to dinner, Riley grabbed a drumstick and dug in. I glanced at Mom, she smiled. Dad cleared his throat loudly. Riley stopped chewing and looked at him.

"Would you like to say the blessing, Erich?" Dad asked, but he was looking at Riley.

"Sure," I said. Riley set down his drumstick. He looked around as if he wasn't sure what was happening. Mom and Dad bowed their heads, so Riley did the same thing.

"Dear Lord," I prayed. "Thank you for this food, and bless it to our bodies. And thank you for bringing us a guest tonight. Amen."

Riley opened his eyes a few seconds after the rest of us. He glanced around the table anxiously. Just to be on the safe side, he waited until Mom took a forkful of mashed potatoes before he snatched up the drumstick and chowed down again.

When Mom and Dad went upstairs to bed, Riley and I stayed down in the living room with the television turned down low. Riley insisted that we watch the movies with no lights on. Every few minutes, lightning struck outside, lighting the room up blue and making me jump nearly out of my skin. Sky stayed close by all night, which was fine with me.

"So how is watching all these movies going to help?" I asked Riley as *Midnight Madness* rewound in the VCR. "How is watching a bunch of dumb movies going to prove whether or not Bigfoot exists?" Both of us were sitting on the carpet leaning against the sofa. Sky was curled up between us.

"Because it shows us how monsters operate," he said. "For one thing, they always show up when the hero and his sidekick are alone—especially if it's the middle of the night and there's a big storm." He gestured toward the window as if to show that the stage was set for a monster to appear.

"Have I mentioned that you watch too much TV?" I asked him.

"Anyway, in every one of these movies, no one believes the hero until it's almost too late," Riley went on. "And the hero and the sidekick are the only ones who see the monster but don't get eaten—except sometimes the sidekick gets eaten near the end."

"You realize these are monster movies and not documentaries, don't you?" I teased him.

Riley ignored me. "And finally the hero,"—he glanced in my direction—"and his sidekick, have to take matters into their own hands and save the town from the monster. And then—"

"*Wait a minute,*" I said. "Wait *one* minute. Which one of us is the sidekick?"

"The sidekick is the one who always interrupts with stupid questions," Riley said pointedly.

"It was *my* dog who found the skeleton," I reminded him. "*I* should be the hero."

Riley ignored me again. "What we really need here is a good title," he told me.

"A title?"

"Yeah," he said. "Like *Revenge of the Bigfoots*."

"*Bigfeet*," I corrected him for the umpteenth time. "And what do we need a title for? This is real life, not one of your stupid monster movies."

"How about *Something Evil in McCreeville?*"

"How about *My Best Friend is an Idiot?*" I suggested, just as the VCR spat out the rewound tape.

Next, we watched *Terror Picnic* and *Fangs*. And then we started *Bride of the Iguana Man*. They were pretty stupid, but things kept jumping out and scaring people, and there was all kinds of creepy music. I hadn't watched as many monster movies as Riley, so I wasn't used to them. A couple of times I actually got so scared I closed my eyes.

The lightning came more frequently as the night wore on, and the thunder got louder—so all in all I was pretty nervous. Sky lay on the floor beside me. Each time the thunder rumbled over the house, he whimpered and nudged himself closer to me. I knew just how he felt.

Riley finished off the third bag of popcorn. He crumpled it into a ball. "There's nothing like a monster movie marathon to give a guy an appetite," he said. "How about putting another bag in the microwave?"

To tell the truth, I would have loved more popcorn—I'd only managed to get a couple of handfuls all night because Riley kept hogging it—but I wasn't in the mood to go in the dark kitchen alone. "You've had enough popcorn," I told Riley. "And you had *two* dinners tonight. Don't you ever get full?"

"Not that I remember," he told me. "Come on; just one more bag. You and me are doing some serious research here. We could *both* use some more."

"You and *I*," I corrected him. "And if you want some, why don't you go make it yourself?"

"Some host you are," Riley said. He pushed the pause button on the remote control and stood up. "Just show me where the popcorn is, and I'll nuke us up a bunch."

I made a point of groaning loudly when I stood up—like it was a big imposition—but I was secretly happy that Riley would be going into the kitchen and turning on some lights. "Why don't we make *two* bags," I suggested. "That way I might actually get to eat some."

Sky followed us to the threshold of the dark kitchen, but wouldn't cross from carpet to tile. He whimpered, pricked up his ears, and then turned and trotted back into the living room with his tail tucked between his legs. I looked in the dark kitchen. All I could see were the glowing blue numbers on the microwave's clock: 1:13.

I waved Riley into the kitchen ahead of me. "The light switch is over next to the refrigerator," I told him. A second later the kitchen was flooded with wonderful, reassuring light.

I stood blinking a moment, happy to be in a well-lit room at last. Riley opened the refrigerator and squatted down to see what was inside. "The popcorn's up *here*," I told him, opening the cupboard. "It doesn't need refrigeration."

Riley stood up straight and closed the refrigerator door. He seemed a little embarrassed. "I was just checking to make sure it was set on the right temperature," he said. "I wasn't going to eat anything."

"*Sure*," I said. I tossed him a bag of unpopped popcorn. "Now why don't you check the settings on the microwave?"

Riley pushed the buttons, and the microwave rattled and buzzed. In a few seconds, the kernels of corn began to pop. Riley turned his back on the kitchen counter and hopped up so he was sitting on it. A flash of lightning flickered in the kitchen window behind him.

He yawned and rubbed the back of his neck. "A couple more movies and you'll be up to speed on monsters," Riley said.

"You know this is really dumb," I told him. "It's not like these movies are educational."

"Of *course* they're educational," Riley said. "You're good at spelling and grammar and that kind of stuff—well this is *my* area of expertise."

I grinned and shook my head. "There's nothing like being an expert in something completely useless," I told him.

"*Useless?!*" Riley sputtered. "Okay, Smart Guy, how do you kill a werewolf?"

I shrugged. Like I said, I don't go in much for horror. I took a stab at it. "Garlic?" I guessed.

"*Garlic?*" Riley snorted. "Werewolves eat garlic for breakfast!" He shook his head and sighed, like he couldn't believe I could be so stupid. "The only way to kill a werewolf is with a silver bullet."

I laughed. I was beginning to relax. "Now *that's* information that's bound to come in handy."

Riley grinned. "You won't be laughing if a werewolf gets loose around here and you start throwing garlic at it," he said. "Admit it—in the event of a monster attack, I'm the only thing standing between this town and total destruction."

I was still laughing when, for some reason, I looked up at the small window above Riley's head. A flash of lightning lit up a furry face and two very human eyes. They stared directly at me through the high window—from at least eight feet off the ground!

My mouth fell open. I felt the blood drain from my face. I backed up until I was pressed against the oven door. I'd entirely lost the power of speech. All I could do was point a shaky finger above Riley's head at the window where the two eyes still glowed in the darkness like embers.

Riley bolted off the counter and turned to look up at the window. "What is it?" Riley asked, suddenly serious. "What's the matter with you?" The eyes blazed red a moment in the darkness and then turned away. The window was empty again.

"D-D-Did you see that?" I managed to say.

"See what?" Riley said. "I didn't see anything. What are you talking about?"

"Eyes," I said. "It was looking in at us."

"What was?"

"Bigfoot," I told him. "I saw it. It was huge."

"You saw a Bigfoot?"

"What else could it have been?"

"It was probably your own reflection," Riley said.

"Yeah, right," I told him. "Look how high that window is. There's no way it was my reflection."

"Well maybe it was your imagination."

I couldn't believe it. I'd just seen a Bigfoot, and Riley—of *all* people—was telling me I'd imagined it! "Look, don't go getting skeptical on me," I told him. "I *know* what I saw. And besides, skeptics are always the first ones eaten."

"Wow," Riley said, looking very impressed. "See, the movies worked. You're finally picking this stuff up."

Riley reached over and switched off the kitchen light. We were plunged into darkness again. The only illumination was the eerie blue light from the microwave.

"Hey, what are you doing?" I shouted. "Turn that back on." My heart was pounding like a jackhammer.

"*Shhhh,*" Riley hissed in the dark. "If the light's off, it won't be able to see inside—but *we* can see out." Riley climbed up and knelt on the kitchen counter in front of the microwave. A flash of lightning silhouetted his head in the window. "I think it's gone," he said. "I don't see anything out there."

That wasn't good enough. I was terrified. I wanted to know it was gone for sure. "Why don't you go outside and make *sure* it's gone?" I suggested. "I'll stay in here and call for help if you get in any trouble."

"What do you mean: Why don't *I* go outside?" Riley sputtered. "Why don't *you* go see, if you're so curious?"

"Because *I'm* just the sidekick," I reminded him. "*You're* the hero. *You're* the one who's supposed to do this kind of thing." I started to plead with him. "Come on, Riley. Just open the door. Just look outside. You want some garlic or something? Mom's got some around here somewhere."

"What *is* it with you and garlic?" Riley asked in the dark. "That's exclusively for vampires."

"Well, what do you use for Bigfeet?" I asked.

Riley shrugged. "You've got me," he said. "The field of Bigfootology is still in its infancy. But I'm pretty sure garlic would just tick him off."

We tiptoed to the back door and looked out the window. I prayed I wouldn't see a pair of eyes looking back in at me. With all the rain, it was hard to see much of anything—but a sudden flash of lightning lit up the yard. I saw the open back gate blowing in the wind.

"You know, I'm sure I closed that thing when I came through," Riley said.

"Yeah," I told him. "You did. I remember making sure."

Riley unlocked the back door and pulled it open a crack. My heart pounded faster. He opened it a little more and stuck his head out. I felt the cold damp air on my face.

"Maybe we *should* look around outside," Riley said. "Maybe we should get some flashlights and look for footprints before the rain washes them all away. We could take pictures this time."

Now that Riley was willing to go outside, it didn't sound like such a hot idea after all—especially since he wanted me to go with him. "No way," I said. "Weren't you paying attention? That's exactly what that guy with the beard said in *Bride of the Iguana Man*. Two minutes later, he was lizard food."

Riley pulled his head inside the door again and looked at me, more impressed than ever. "Good thinking," he said. "You're learning the way of the monster."

"Good," I said. "Does that mean we can stop watching those stupid movies?"

# Chapter 7

I didn't get a minute of sleep. The two of us spent the whole night in the living room. The thunder and lightning stopped about three in the morning, and the rain stopped about an hour later. After that, the only sound was Riley's snoring as he slept on the sofa, and the constant dripping outside. I put on Mom's video of *The Wizard of Oz* to help me relax, but I was so on edge I had to fast-forward through the scene with the flying monkeys.

Then the words from Deuteronomy came to me again: "The Lord himself goes before you and will be with you; he will never leave you nor forsake you. Do not be afraid; do not be discouraged." I patted the ground next to my leg and a sleepy Sky came over and plopped down beside me. I scratched behind his ears and bowed my head.

When daylight appeared in the living room window, I pulled back the curtains and looked around outside. Except for the open gate, I didn't see any evidence of what happened last night.

I went over to the sofa and shook Riley. "Quit it," he groaned and rolled over. I shook him again. "Come on, Mom," he said. "It's Saturday; I don't have to get up for school."

"It's *Sunday*," I told him. "And I'm not your mother."

Riley rolled on his back and sat up. Half his face was red and he had drool in the corner of his mouth. He looked around groggily. "Where am I?"

"Oz," I told him. "A tornado came through last night. You should look outside; everything's in color."

Riley scratched his head and looked around again. "We're at *your* house," he informed me—as if I didn't know. "Say, did you see a Bigfoot last night or was that a dream?"

"It was no dream," I told him.


Ten minutes later, we were hunting through the dripping back yard looking for footprints. I'd brought my camera in case we found anything. There was no telling when a new storm might sweep in and erase any footprints we found. But the heavy rains had wiped away any marks in the mud.

Sky stood in the kitchen doorway watching us. His tail was wagging, but he held his head low. He looked like he wanted to come outside and join us, but it was as if he was chained to the spot. He wouldn't budge from the doorway.

"It's OK, boy," I told him. "You stay right there. We'll be back in a minute."

I went around the side of the house and looked up at the kitchen window. It was higher off the ground than I had imagined—you'd have to be nine or ten feet tall to peek into the kitchen! I looked down at the ground where the monster must have stood. It was a big puddle of brown water—there was no hope of finding footprints there.

I shook my head. It seemed hopeless that we'd ever convince anyone. Riley was over by the back gate inspecting the latch. He seemed oddly cheerful. "This is pointless," I told him. "We're never going to find anything. Everyone in school thinks we're insane, and we're never going to prove them wrong."

Riley grinned at me. "Relax, dude," he said. "This always happens."

"What always happens?"

"*This*," he said, sweeping his arm out to include the whole backyard—maybe even the construction site and woods on the other side of the fence. "No one ever believes the hero and the sidekick until the movie's almost over."

I groaned. "Couldn't we just fast-forward this movie a little?" I asked him. "Couldn't we find some proof *now?* I'm ready to have people believe us. I'm ready to get on with my life."

"We don't even have a title yet, and you want this movie to end?" Riley said smiling.

I just stared at him. Why couldn't he ever behave like a normal person? He pulled the gate shut. "How about *An Appointment with Terror?*" he said. "How's that for a title?"

"How about an appointment with a psychologist?" I suggested. "You're not playing with a full deck."

"You're not being a very good host," a voice said behind me. Mom was standing in the doorway with Sky. Her hands were on her hips. "How was last night's sleepover?"

I glanced over at Riley. I was hoping he wasn't going to blurt out anything about my seeing Bigfoot in the kitchen window. He just shrugged.

"We had a good time," I told Mom.

74

"Well, why don't you both wash up for break-fast," Mom told us. "Riley, will you be coming with us to church?"

Riley shrugged. "Does it cost anything?" he asked. He scratched his neck. He didn't seem very excited about the prospect of attending church.

Mom smiled. "No," she said. "Why don't you call your mom and make sure it's OK, and then you can have lunch with us afterwards."

At the word *lunch*, Riley's attitude changed. "Sounds great," he said. "I'll call my mom."


We were the first ones in my Sunday school room. I picked two chairs in the middle and we sat down. Riley fidgeted while we waited for the others to show up. All the kids in my Sunday school class go to my school, so I wasn't sure what they'd think when they saw me there with Riley. I was hoping there would be no jokes about Bigfoot.

"Are they going to make me do anything?" Riley asked me suddenly. He seemed a little nervous.

I grinned. "Is this *really* the first time you've ever been to church?" I asked him. It was a little hard to believe.

"Yep," he said. "This is the first time you ever *asked* me to come." He was right, and the smile disappeared from my face.

In a few minutes, the room was crowded with the other kids. They seemed very amused to see Riley and me sitting together. I heard a lot of whispering. I thought I heard someone say "monster" and "loony," but I couldn't be sure.

Riley kept changing positions in his chair. He seemed awkward and nervous. I suppose church *might* seem a little scary if you'd never been there before.

About five minutes after the class was supposed to begin, the teacher still hadn't arrived. I was disappointed. Glen, our junior high leader, was a cool guy. If anyone could put Riley at ease, it would be him. I glanced up at the clock and then around at the other kids. They all seemed to be watching Riley and me.

*We can get through this*, I thought. *We'll be fine as long as Riley can keep his mouth shut for the next hour.* I glanced over at him. He was so uneasy he could barely breathe, let alone talk. *No problem*, I told myself. *What are the chances that the subject of Bigfoot will come up in Sunday school?*

The door at the front of the room swung open, and Mr. Simpson, the Sunday school superintendent, leaned into the room.

"Glen came down with the flu this morning," Mr. Simpson announced from the doorway. "So we've asked one of the other teachers to fill in just for today."

Mr. Simpson stepped aside and Miss Kathy, who usually taught the second graders, stepped into the room. She was only five or six years older than us, and she was shorter than most of the boys. She looked a little nervous at the prospect of being in front of a bunch of junior highers. She gripped a Bible and a paperback book in her hands as she walked to the front of the room, like she was afraid we might try to take them from her.

When Mr. Simpson left the room, Miss Kathy had us read today's Bible chapter out loud. We were starting a new lesson book on the Old Testament, and the chapter we read was Genesis 1.

Usually, Glen read the chapter to us aloud while we followed along in our own Bibles—but Miss Kathy seemed too nervous to control her voice, so she asked for volunteers to read out loud.

When we were done reading the chapter, Miss Kathy looked up and asked if we had any questions. I could tell by the terrified look on her face that she was praying everything was crystal clear. One of the kids raised his hand. Miss Kathy took a sudden breath and pointed at him. You would've thought she was in front of a firing squad.

"What about dinosaurs?" the boy asked. "Did God create *them?*"

Miss Kathy looked down at her lesson book. It was clear there was nothing in there about dinosaurs. Beads of sweat appeared on her forehead. She was badly flustered, but she tried her best to hide it.

Riley, on the other hand, began to relax. Seeing Miss Kathy so nervous seemed to make him less anxious.

"Yes, I guess so," Miss Kathy said, after a long, embarrassing pause. "God created everything—but some things have gone extinct."

"Like the dodo?" someone said, trying to be helpful.

Miss Kathy didn't say anything. She flipped to the back of the book to see if there was an index. There wasn't. She ran a finger around the inside of her collar. "I guess so," she said at last. "God created every animal—it says so right here: 'God created the wild animals, each according to their kinds.'"

I felt sorry for Miss Kathy. She was definitely out of her depth with junior highers. She seemed terrified of us.

"Any more questions?" she asked. I glanced around the room. Everyone looked down at the open Bibles in their laps. We were all as embarrassed as she was. It looked like everyone was going to take it easy on her. There would be no more questions.

Riley sat up straight and looked around. He slowly raised his hand. I moaned and sank down in my chair.

"No," I whispered out of the side of my mouth. "Don't say anything about—"

But it was too late; Miss Kathy pointed at Riley's raised hand. "Do you have a question?" she asked.

Riley cleared his throat. "What's your position on big, hairy, human-like ape creatures?" he asked.

I slapped my forehead with my hand. By lunch time on Monday, it would be all over school.

When we got back home after church, Riley couldn't wait for lunch. As soon as the front door opened and he smelled the roast beef Mom had left in the oven, he was ready to eat. He was practically drooling on himself.

It's my job to set the table, so I asked Riley to clear some stuff off the table while I got out the plates and silverware. He was glad to help if it meant that lunch would come a few minutes faster. I came back into the dining room with four plates and utensils. I set them on the table and started arranging things.

Riley picked up the Bibles that Mom, Dad, and I had set on the table when we came in from church. He put them on the sideboard. He picked up my camera and turned to put it on the sideboard too. Suddenly, he stopped and looked down at the camera like he'd never seen one before.

"It's a *cam–er–a*," I told him, pronouncing each syllable distinctly. "We use it to take pictures."

Riley ignored my teasing and continued to examine the camera in his hand. "This is exactly what we need," Riley said. He raised the camera to his eye and looked at me through the lens. "Does it have a flash?"

"A flash?" I said, arranging the last piece of silverware on the table. "Why do we need a flash?" In the pit of my stomach I already suspected the answer.

"Because Bigfoot is nocturnal," Riley said. "It only seems to come out at night. That's why it's been able to hide in these woods for so long without anyone knowing. We're going to need the flash if we're going to take its picture tonight."

"Tonight?" I didn't like the direction this conversation was going.

"Sure," Riley said. "We can get its picture when it shows up to raid your trash cans."

"How are we going to do that?" I asked him.

"Easy," Riley said. "One of us will hide in the trash can. And then when the Sasquatch takes off the lid, you'll pop out of the trash can and snap his picture."

I put my hands on my hips. "*I* pop out and take his picture?" I said.

"You're smaller than I am," Riley pointed out. "I'd never fit in one of those cans. Besides, I have a fear of closed places."

"Hello?" I said. "I have a fear of *giant hairy monsters*. I'm not setting foot out of this house tonight."

"Well, if you have a better idea of how to prove that there's a Bigfoot out there, I'd like to hear it."

"I *do* have a better idea," I said. It had just come to me while we were talking. "Let's just leave out a trash can as bait, and rig up the camera on my tripod so that it takes a picture when someone opens the lid."

Riley looked at me and stroked his chin. "It's not as daring as my plan," Riley said.

"It's also not as stupid," I pointed out.

Riley sighed. "OK," he said. "We'll try it your way."

After lunch, Riley went to the grocery store to buy some bananas. He seemed to think that putting bananas in the trash can would be a good way to lure Bigfoot—because in every Bigfoot movie he'd ever seen, the monster looked like a gorilla. I could have pointed out that a wild Bigfoot would have to hike a long way through the state of Washington before he found a banana tree, but I kept my mouth shut. I wanted Riley out of my hair for a while. I wanted an hour on my own so I could rig up some kind of trigger on the camera without him hovering over my shoulder making dumb comments.

I found a thick rubber band and slipped it over the body of the camera so that it held down the shutter release button. Then I found a cap to an old marker and tied a string firmly around the middle. I stretched the rubber band back and put the pen cap over the shutter release button. When I pulled on the string, the cap sprung out from under the rubber band, and the rubber band snapped down on the shutter button. The camera flashed. It was simple, but it worked quite well.

I thought if we tied the other end of the string to the trash can lid, and put the camera on the tripod behind Dad's woodpile where it wouldn't be so noticeable, it should snap a photo as soon as someone lifted the lid off the trash can.

When Riley got back from the grocery store with his bananas, we tested the set-up. Riley insisted on playing the part of Bigfoot. He jogged fifty yards toward the woods and then ambled back, scratching himself under the arms and occasionally beating his chest with his fists. He was eerily gorilla-like.

"Is this really necessary?" I asked him. "Couldn't you just pull the lid off the can? I really want to see if this will work."

Riley ignored me. He arrived at the trash can and squatted in front of it in ape-like fashion. He looked at it a long time, tilting his head to one side, not comprehending. I glanced at my wristwatch. He was driving me crazy.

Riley sniffed at the air, like he had just detected the sweet scent of bananas. He slowly reached for the trash can lid and then suddenly drew his arm back, like he sensed it was a trap. I couldn't take it anymore. I wanted to strangle him. "Just grab the stupid lid," I shouted. "Just reach out and grab the lid."

Riley reached out his gorilla arm and snatched the lid from the trash can. The string plucked out the marker cap, and the rubber band snapped down. The camera flashed.

Riley stood up straight and grinned. "Hey, that's not bad," he said looking down at the lid he was holding. "This might really work. With *your* brain and *my* acting, we make quite a team."

"Acting?" I said.

# Chapter 8

A soon as I woke up the next morning, I remembered how we'd set up the camera the day before, just as the sun was going down. I dove out of bed and pulled on my clothes, ran downstairs and out the back door. I was halfway across the yard when I noticed I wasn't wearing any shoes. I didn't care. I flung open the back gate and saw the scattered trash cans. Pieces of banana skin and smashed banana meat were trampled into the grass. It was a wonderful thing to see. *What do you know,* I thought. *Riley was right: Bigfeet really do like bananas!*

I ran over to the wood pile to get the camera. If the rubber band was tight around the button, it would mean we had succeeded—we'd have an actual photo of Bigfoot!

But behind the woodpile all I found was the tripod lying on its side with two broken legs. The camera was gone!

I ran inside and dialed Riley's number on the kitchen phone. I was angry. That camera was a Christmas present from my grandparents. It cost over a hundred dollars. It had an automatic zoom lens and everything.

"Did it take a picture?" Riley wanted to know as soon as he recognized my voice.

"No," I said. "It took my whole camera."

"Huh?"

"The monster," I said. "It stole my camera."

"You sure?" Riley asked.

"Of course," I said. "You know what was on top of the tripod this morning when I went outside?"

"What?"

"*Nothing*," I shouted. "That's what I'm talking about."

"It's got to be *somewhere*," Riley told me.

"What a brilliant observation," I said. "Of *course* it's *some*where."

Riley was silent a moment. I knew he was thinking, or at least trying to. "A big, hairy monster doesn't need a camera," he said at last.

"Another stroke of genius," I said. "How do you do it?"

"Look, Erich," Riley said. "Don't be so snippy. We'll find your camera. We'll develop the film. And when we do, it will probably have a whole family of Bigfeet posing and saying cheese."

"How are we going to find the camera?"

"The Sasquatch must have left some kind of trail," Riley said. "We'll follow the trail until we find the camera."

"A trail?"

"Yeah," Riley said. "Broken twigs and scraps of fur—that kind of stuff. Indian scouts are always following that sort of thing in the movies."

I held the phone away from my ear and looked at it. I put it back to my ear. "You watch *westerns* too?"

"Dude, I watch *everything*," Riley said. "I'm well-rounded."

Riley arrived at my back gate to walk to school. We hiked along the narrow alley made by the construction site fence and the back fences of the houses on my street. Inside the construction site, work had already begun for the day, but the fence was so high we couldn't tell what they were building inside. You couldn't even see over it from my second-story bedroom window. It was some big secret, but of course I had other things on my mind.

"Right after school," Riley said. "Right after school, we'll head out into the woods while there's still light, and we'll find your camera."

"You sound very optimistic," I told him. "That's a big forest. What makes you think we'll ever see that camera again?"

"Because the exact same thing happened in *Loch Ness Nightmare*," Riley said. "Except the camera was underwater, and they had to go scuba diving to find it. We're *bound* to find it. It's *got* to be easier on dry ground."

I just sighed.


Riley and I split up as soon as we went through the school's front doors. His locker is on the first floor and mine is on the second. Riley's my best friend, but to tell you the truth, it was a relief to get away from him. As I climbed the stairs, I was deep in my own thoughts. Since the afternoon we found the skeleton, my life had taken a turn for the worse. I hadn't had a good night's sleep. I couldn't concentrate at school. It was like I had the weight of the world on my shoulders.

I got to the top of the steps and headed down the hall. It suddenly dawned on me that everyone in the hallway was silent. They were all watching me. At the other end of the hall, I noticed something large and white hanging from my locker. When I got closer, I saw that it was a huge sheet of foam rubber cut in the shape of a foot and taped firmly to my locker door. It had ODOR EATER printed along the top. Beneath that was a note in handwriting:

> Here's the proof
> you've been looking for.
> —XOXOXO Bigfoot

I heard giggling behind me. It felt like everyone in the hall was watching me. I felt my face grow red. I peeled the giant Odor Eater off my locker and let it fall to the tile floor. I twisted the dial on my lock—though, at that moment, I couldn't even think what my combination was. The bell rang, and I heard the shuffling of feet behind me as everyone cleared the hallway and headed off to their classes.

By the time I got my locker open and found my math book, I was late for class.

When we got back to my house that afternoon after school, Riley insisted we head immediately into the woods to look for the camera. We paused outside my back gate.

"Wait here," I told him. "I'm going to get my pellet gun before we head into the woods."

Riley snorted. "What good is a pellet gun against a ten-foot tall Sasquatch?" he asked.

I shrugged. "I'm just hoping the pellets annoy him enough that he eats you instead of me," I told him.

"Funny," Riley said. "How about we bring Sky too? Maybe he can sniff out a trail."

"Nah," I said. "He won't come. I can barely get him to go outside at all these days."

I went inside and got my pellet gun from my bedroom. When I came downstairs, Sky was curled up asleep in a rectangle of sunlight that shone through the living room window onto the carpet. He looked peaceful and calm. I just let him lie there. I went back outside. Riley was looking at the broken tripod behind the woodpile.

"You ready to go?" he asked.

I looked out at the woods. "You *sure* Bigfoot is asleep?" I asked him. "Remember, the science of Bigfootology is still in its infancy."

Riley rubbed the back of his neck. "Pretty sure," he said. "You still want to do this?"

I looked down at the ground. I was scared. But I thought of the giant Odor Eater on my locker and all the laughing behind my back at school. Riley had always been the class clown—he was a character—but I suspected he didn't like being laughed at any more than I did.

"You think we'll really find the camera?" I asked him. "You think we really got his picture when he lifted the trash can lid?"

"I don't know," Riley admitted. "But there's only one way to find out."

I looked back at my house and then out at the woods again. "Lead the way," I told him.

Riley and I headed along the edge of the construction site fence. A path was worn in the grass from all the people who had walked around the fence, trying to get a peek inside. There were all kinds of rumors flying through town about what was being built, but no one knew for sure.

On the other side of the fence, deep in the fenced-off area, we heard the constant clanging and wheezing of big machinery. We left the fence and the noise behind us as we headed deep into the pine forest. Then all we heard was the unsettling silence of the woods.

Riley and I had spent a lot of time in these woods. Each time we hit a fork in the familiar trails, Riley would flip a coin and head down one path or the other. Every once in a while, I heard something moving deep in the forest. It could have been any-thing—a squirrel, a marmot, a monster.

"Where's the farthest you've ever been in these woods?" Riley asked me.

"I went camping with my dad once," I told him. "We went all the way to Bear Mountain. The trip took three days."

"See any bears on Bear Mountain?" Riley wanted to know.

"Nah," I said. "It's just a name. Dad said there hasn't been a bear in these parts since *he* was a kid. They've moved way up north."

"Seems like the mountain needs a new name," Riley told me. "It should be named for something that really lives out here."

"Like Bigfoot Mountain?"

"That's what I was thinking," Riley said.

An hour-and-a-half later, the daylight began to dim, but we hadn't found any trace of Bigfoot or the camera. We'd have to turn around and head back soon. I sure didn't want to be in these woods after sundown.

We stopped at a fork in the trail. Riley pulled the quarter from the pocket of his jeans. "Heads or tails?"

"I thought you were going to track Bigfoot through these woods like the Indians on TV," I told

Riley. "And here we are flipping coins. I guess for once TV let you down."

Riley didn't say anything. He seemed discouraged. He wasn't his usually upbeat, enthusiastic self.

"If this *was* a movie, we'd have found the camera by now," I told him. "It would just be sitting in the middle of the trail, and we'd walk right up to it. That's the problem with movies. Things are too easy."

Riley didn't say anything. He flipped the coin and we headed down the path on the right. Maybe I was getting through to him.

"It's like those cop movies in New York," I told him. "They always pull up and find an empty parking space right in front of the building. But in real life, they'd be driving around for a half-hour just looking for an open space."

Riley didn't say anything, so I went on talking. "It's insulting to our intelligence," I told him. "Real life isn't like the movies."

Riley stopped walking, so I did too.

"In real life, things don't always work out perfectly," I told him. "You don't just find cameras lying in the middle of the path."

"You mean like that?" Riley said.

"Huh?"

Riley pointed to the ground ahead of us. There, right in the middle of the trail, sat my camera. It looked dusty and banged up, but it was in one piece. I looked at Riley and back at the camera. "How did you *do* that?" I asked him.

Riley just took a deep breath and smiled. "Television," he said, full of inspiration. "Is it *ever* wrong?"

I groaned and shook my head. I'd never hear the end of this. Riley walked over to the camera and picked it up. He held it up to his chin and blew off some dust. "How do you get the film out of this thing?"

"Just give it here," I told him. "You're really ticking me off."

Riley handed me the camera. "What are *you* so angry about?"

"You and your stupid movies," I told him. I pushed the button on the bottom of the camera and started cranking the film back into its canister. "Why can't you ever read a book for a change?"

Riley grinned. "Nothing this cool *ever* happens in books," he told me.

I unlatched the back of the camera and shook the film canister into my palm. It looked OK. I slipped it into the pocket of my jeans and checked the camera to see if it still worked. I clicked the shutter a few times. It was dirty and scratched, but it seemed OK.

We headed back through the woods. "If this was one of your stupid movies, what would we do now?" I asked Riley.

"We'd go to the one-hour photo place on Park Street," he said. "And then we take the photo of the monster to the authorities."

"Yeah?" I said. "And then what happens?"

Riley scratched his head. "Well, in most movies they *still* wouldn't believe us," he said.

I stopped walking. "Well, then, what's the point?" I wanted to know. "Why did we *do* all this? Why did we come all the way out here looking for the stupid camera?"

Riley looked at me and shook his head. "This isn't a movie," he informed me. "This is real life."

I could have strangled him.

# Chapter 9

The one-hour photo shop took only a half hour to develop our film. When the clerk handed me the envelope, Riley tore it out of my hands and ran outside, leaving me to pay. I paid the clerk and followed Riley out onto the sidewalk.

"What *is* all this stuff?" Riley said, flipping through the photos.

I looked over his shoulder. "That's my trip to Seattle," I told him. He flipped past a picture of me at Pike's Street Market and one of Mom and me on a ferry.

"That's me in front of the Space Needle," I told him. "Slow down."

"Needle schmeedle," he said. "Where's the monster?"

He got to the last picture in the stack of photos. It looked like it was in black and white, even though all the other photos were color.

He turned the picture sideways and then upside down. "What *is* it?" he said.

I studied the photo over his shoulder. "It's fur," I told him. "It looks like black fur. And it looks like there's bluish skin underneath." I pulled the hand holding the photo closer to my eyes. "Look," I said, "You can see part of the fence in the background. It's definitely the monster."

Riley tilted his head to one side. "I think it's his shoulder," he said. "See? Right here you can see part of his arm."

I tilted my head too. Riley was right. The photo was out of focus, but it was definitely a huge, hairy, muscular shoulder. Under the fur the skin was blue-white.

"OK, so it isn't suitable for framing," I said. "But they've *got* to believe us now."


Mayor Picket leaned back in his chair to catch the late afternoon light from the window behind him. He held the photo close to his nose. He laughed. "This is your monster?" he said. "It could be a close-up of my wife's mink coat for all *I* can tell."

"Not unless she was out raiding Erich's trash cans last night," Riley said.

The smile disappeared from the mayor's face. He set the photo down on his desk and slid it across to Riley. It was clear he didn't like having his wife accused of raiding the garbage. "What I'm saying is that it could be anything," he told us. He leaned forward and looked us over. "Including some kind of practical joke."

"This is no joke," I said.

"I seem to recall someone supergluing a pair of sunglasses on the statue of Thaddeus McCree in the park," the mayor said.

"*You* were the one who did that?" I asked Riley.

Riley nodded. UFO reports. Practical jokes. Why didn't I ever hear about this stuff?

"OK," Riley said. "I admit I've pulled a few pranks. But this photo is on the level."

The mayor leaned back in his chair. "Look, boys," he said. "I happen to know there's a rational explanation for everything that's happened. We're in the middle of a project that could make McCreeville a major tourist destination. The last thing we need is for you two to start a panic."

I glanced over at Riley and back at the mayor. "Sir," I said. "Shouldn't we do something just to be on the safe side?"

The mayor sat back in his chair and rested his hands on his belly. "Boys, why don't you two just stop worrying about the well-being of McCreeville," he said. "After all, that's *my* job."

When we got outside, the streetlights were just beginning to flicker on. Riley and I walked silently along Park Street toward my house on the edge of town. We passed the laundromat and the general store. We passed Clayton's Hardware and Bernie's Cafe. I wondered what would happen to this little town once the Bigfeet started roaming the streets.

"I can't believe he blew us off like that," Riley said. "We had photographic proof."

"We had a photo of some *hair*," I reminded him. "Lots of things have hair. It's hardly proof." We passed Mr. Benson's barbershop.

"It isn't fair," Riley said. "Because of the mayor, everyone in this town is in danger."

We passed the *Weekly Sentinel* office on the far side of the street. The light was still on inside.

Riley stopped walking. "If we could take this picture directly to the people, then maybe we'd get some results," Riley said. He headed across the street to the newspaper office.

Riley pushed the door open and went inside. I followed. The room was dimly lit and smelled of ink. Mr. Nestor stood up but didn't come out from behind his desk. He was finishing up tomorrow's newspaper and his desk was cluttered with papers.

"What can I do for you boys?" he wanted to know. "You looking for a newspaper route?"

"No," Riley told him, holding out his hand for Mr. Nestor to shake. "We're here to offer you the scoop of your life." Mr. Nestor glanced over at me and then shook Riley's hand. He wasn't sure what we were up to.

"Scoop?" he said.

"What's your front page story?" Riley asked.

"It's about the damaged shuffleboard deck and the teen tournament going on tomorrow," Mr. Nestor said. "I thought it might help them raise funds for repairs."

Riley looked over at me and grinned. "Well, stop the presses," he said. "We've got a story here that'll blow shuffleboard off the front page." Riley slapped the photo down on Mr. Nestor's desk. "Photographic proof that Bigfoot exists," he announced dramatically.

Mr. Nestor picked up the photo and studied it. "You say this is a Bigfoot?" he asked.

"We snapped the picture ourselves," Riley told him. "We're the ones who found the skeleton."

Mr. Nestor rubbed his chin and nodded, his brow furrowed in thought. "Maybe I can use it, boys," he said. "I don't have a good photo for the front page. How did you say you got this picture?"

The next morning, I woke up when my alarm clock went off. I sat up in bed feeling hopeful. The McCreeville *Weekly Sentinel* would be on the doorstep. It would have the photo of Bigfoot on the front page. It would clear our names. We'd go to school as heroes instead of school jokes.

I got dressed and went downstairs. I opened the front door and spied the paper on the front porch. *This is it*, I thought. All the snide gossip and laughter would stop the minute I opened today's paper. I'd be respected again. I could hold my head high at school.

Mom and Dad hadn't come downstairs yet, so I had the kitchen to myself. I poured myself a bowl of cereal and sat down at the table. Taking a deep breath, I unfolded the paper.

There it was on the front page—our picture of Bigfoot! It was wonderful to see. It took up almost the whole top half of the page! It wasn't as clear as the original, but you could still make out that unmistakable muscular shoulder. I felt jubilant—like I might float up off the kitchen chair into the air.

I glanced at the big headline across the top of the page:

LOCAL LADS NOT PLAYING WITH FULL DECK

*What!?*

I couldn't believe it! How could nice old Mr. Nestor mock us like this? Everyone in town thought we were crazy, but he didn't have to make it official by putting it on the front page. My face stung with embarrassment.

I read the caption below the photo: *Riley Hope and Erich DeHart claim to have snapped this photo of Bigfoot near the new construction site.* I looked back at the insulting headline. It didn't seem like Mr. Nestor. It was so unfair.

Then it dawned on me. On the left side of the front page was a narrow article that had nothing to do with our Bigfoot photo. It was about the damaged shuffleboard deck and the tournament that would take place this afternoon—Local Lads Not Playing With Full Deck.

I laid my head down on the cool kitchen table. The headline wasn't about Riley and me—but how many other people in town would make the same mistake I did?

The phone rang. I went to the counter and looked down at the phone. I didn't want to answer it, but I didn't want Mom or Dad to pick it up either. I took a deep breath, grabbed the receiver, and put it to my ear.

"Hello?" I said into the mouthpiece, expecting the worst.

"Is this Erich DeHart?" a voice asked.

I swallowed. "Yes," I said. "Yes, it is."

"Well, this is Bigfoot," the voice said. "I just called to say I loved the photo. Do you think I could get a wallet-sized copy?" In the background, I could hear muffled laughter. I hung up the phone.

Once I got to school, my day didn't improve at all. Even a couple of the teachers teased me about the photo. All day long, kids in the halls kept handing me playing cards—the four of hearts, the six of clubs, the queen of diamonds. At first, I had no idea what was going on and then it hit me suddenly: Local Lads Not Playing With Full Deck. *Hardy har har.*

Riley and I walked home together, depressed and discouraged. At least there weren't many kids around—they were all over at the other side of town watching the big shuffleboard tournament.

"What do you want to do today?" I asked Riley as we walked along the construction site fence.

"I don't know," he said sullenly. "What do *you* want to do?"

"I was thinking I might move to a new state, get plastic surgery, and start my life over with a new identity," I told him. "I don't know any other way I'll get to lead a normal life again."

"If we had some proof . . ." Riley started to say.

"Give it up," I told him. "Our *proof* was just on the front page of the paper, and look how *that* turned out."

"I mean real proof," Riley said. "A good, sharp photo of Bigfoot."

"And how are we going to get that?"

Riley stopped walking and looked at me. He looked a little pale. "We're going to have to hide in the woods tonight and wait for him to come to your trash cans," Riley said. "It's the only way. He isn't going to come ringing your doorbell."

"We can rig up the camera again," I suggested. "Maybe we'll get a good shot this time."

Riley shook his head. "It's not going to work," he said. "We've got to be there so we can get a good shot. It's the only way we'll convince anyone."

We walked on in silence. I couldn't think of anything to say. I couldn't figure out how to change Riley's mind.

"Imagine it," Riley said. "The McCreeville *Weekly Sentinel* with a big clear photo of a Bigfoot on the front page. No one would dare make fun of us with proof like that."

"Doesn't it seem a little dangerous?" I asked. "What if it gets us?"

"The monster never gets the hero," Riley said. He gave me a weak smile. "We've got to do this, Erich."

"The monster sometimes gets the sidekick," I reminded him.

Riley looked down at the ground and then back at me. "OK," he said softly. "I'll do it on my own. Just give me the camera and show me how to use it. I'll do it for both of us."

I didn't know what to say. I knew that Riley was as scared as I was. But he was willing to risk his life to clear our names and protect our town. He could be a goof sometimes, but in many ways I had to admire him. "No," I said. "We're in this together. I'll do it with you."

"Really?" he said. He looked very relieved.

"Sure," I told him. "I figure that both of us will have to survive so there can be a sequel."

Riley grinned. "*Return to Bigfoot Mountain,*" he said. "In that one, we should have less trouble convincing people."

I waited in the dark in my room for Riley's whistle. I lay in bed with the covers pulled up to my chin. Under the covers, I was wearing all my clothes, including my shoes and my jacket. I had a small flashlight in my pocket. My pellet gun leaned against the wall in the corner by the door. It was loaded and ready.

I had planned not to fall asleep, but when Riley's whistle came from down below my window, I sat up in bed, wondering what was going on. I looked at my alarm clock. It was only 10:15. The whistle came again.

I'd told Riley to whistle when he got there. I told him to imitate a birdcall—that way Mom and Dad would never suspect what was going on. But instead, Riley was standing down in my backyard, loudly whistling some corny song. I slapped my forehead and groaned. I jumped out of bed and ran to the window. I pulled it open. The whistling was even louder now. I could see Riley down there in the moonlight.

"*Shhhhhhh*," I hissed. "Knock it off. You'll wake everyone up." Riley looked up at me from the middle of Mom's rock garden with his lips still puckered. He seemed surprised to see me at the window.

"Sure thing, dude," he said. "*No problema.*"

I just shook my head and closed the window.

I slipped out of my bedroom and downstairs. I stole through the kitchen toward the back door. Before I opened it, I looked out through the glass window. All I could see was my own reflection, so I pressed my face closer. Another face peered in at me. I yelled and flung myself backward onto the kitchen floor before I realized it was just Riley.

I was shaking when I pulled open the back door and slipped down the back steps. I followed Riley out the back gate and closed it behind us. We stood there by the row of trash cans. I could smell bananas. Riley must have already loaded the cans with his bait.

"Dude," Riley whispered once the gate clicked shut. "What did you scream for? You could have woken up your mom and dad."

"*I* could have woken up my mom and dad?" I said. "*You* were standing out in the back yard whistling show tunes."

"That was no show tune," he informed me. "It was the theme to *Bride of the Iguana Man*. And *you* were the one who told me to whistle."

"I said to whistle like *a bird*," I told him. "I didn't tell you to stand out in the yard and entertain the neighborhood with some monster-movie medley."

"You said to whistle like a bird?" Riley asked while leading me over to the stand of trees where we'd agreed to hide. "I don't remember that."

"You never remember *anything*," I scolded him. "You'd forget your own head if it wasn't attached."

"I'm under a lot of stress," he told me. He sat down in a little hollow among the trees where we'd be well hidden. I sat down too. "I don't have your perfect memory," Riley sniffed. "I was out here on my own with the Bigfoots, completely defenseless."

I didn't correct him. But I had a reason. It had just occurred to me, when Riley said the word "defenseless," that my pellet gun was right now propped in the corner of my room. With all my scolding of Riley for forgetting, it didn't seem like the right time to mention that *I'd* forgotten to bring our only means of defense.

Riley and I sat back to back on the pine needle-covered floor of the forest, so nothing could sneak up behind us. Riley sat facing the woods, and I sat facing the row of trash cans. We were near the edge of the forest, so there were only a few trees between me and my back gate. Although it was dark, I could also see quite far along the construction site fence in the moonlight.

Seeing anything in the woods was a different matter. The forest was black and cold, which was pretty creepy. It was also full of sounds, which made it a hundred times scarier. An owl hooted eerily overhead. A raccoon chattered deep among the trees. A coyote yapped and howled off in the distance. Something scampered through the under-brush nearby—there seemed to be creatures moving all around us, but we couldn't see a thing. My eyes darted this way and that. I was nervous and jumpy. My breath caught each time a twig snapped or a branch groaned.

We sat and waited, minute after minute, with our backs pressed together, our eyes and ears straining. Hours into our vigil, my body ached with tiredness, but I wasn't at all sleepy. I was nervous and alert. My eyes were wide open, but I was praying like crazy.

"So tell me more about how God created the world," Riley whispered. "You know, that stuff in Sunday school. That was really cool."

I wasn't sure what Riley wanted to know. "Well, God created the world in six days," I told him. "He just made it out of nothing."

"You think he's still here?"

I wasn't sure if he was talking about God or Bigfoot. "Do I think *who's* still *where?*" I asked him.

"God," Riley said. "You think he's still in the world? You think he's here in these woods?"

"Yeah," I told him. "He's here." The fog swirled and eddied around me. "'The Lord himself goes before you, and will be with you;'" I quoted. "'He will never leave you nor forsake you. Do not be afraid; do not be discouraged.'"

"That's pretty cool," Riley said. "How come you never told me this stuff before? How come you never asked me to come to church?"

I was silent a long time. "I don't know," I told him. "I'm sorry."

We didn't talk for a while. A ground mist began to swirl among the trees, and my face got cold and damp. I turned up my collar. I pulled my knees up to my chin and hugged my legs, trying to stay warm. The mist grew thicker until the trees loomed around us in a ghostly heavy fog. It was so cold, my body trembled uncontrollably—at least I told myself it was because of the cold.

"How about *Terror among the Trees?*" Riley said suddenly. "That would be a pretty good title if this was a movie."

He was right. It was the perfect title, but I didn't say anything. I didn't want to think about horror movies right now. I didn't want to imagine all the things that jump out of the fog in the middle of the night in scary films. I just wanted to think about how God was here with us. I shivered and pressed my back against Riley's. I peered into the deepening gloom and prayed.

"What time do you think it is?" Riley asked me an hour or so later.

"I don't know," I whispered. "Probably around two in the morning." I was tired and achy, but most of all, I was scared. All I wanted was to go inside where it was safe and warm. I tried to think of some good excuse to call off our vigil. "Maybe we should call it a night," I told Riley. "It's late—and even if the monster *did* come, I don't think we could get a photo in all this fog."

Riley sat quietly a few seconds. With our backs pressed together, I could feel him breathing. "Maybe you're right," he said after a long pause. "Maybe we should try again some other night."

I was flooded with relief and thankfulness. Instantly a weight was lifted from my shoulders. I actually smiled. But the smile disappeared when I heard a loud and heavy breathing deep in the fog. My own breath stopped. My ears strained to hear. Nothing.

"Did you hear that?" Riley asked breathlessly.

"Shhhh," I answered.

We sat another moment in silent terror, and then the sound came again. It was in front of me and over to the left. Riley silently scrambled over to my side. He didn't dare have his back to the sound. It was a heavy, wet breathing—so deep and rumbling it made the hair on my neck stand on end.

I stared into the fog. The sound seemed to be moving slowly down along the construction site fence toward the trash cans at my back gate. Soon I heard the heavy, slow thumping of feet—and the sound got louder and louder until I could feel each footstep vibrate in the ground beneath me.

"This is it," Riley said. "Have you got the camera ready?"

To tell the truth, I'd forgotten all about the plan. The only thing running through my mind was the impulse to take off running. I felt around on the damp ground and found the camera. I switched it on with trembling fingers. *Please, God,* I prayed. *Keep us safe.*

The monster was nearly in front of us now, and I thought I could make out a huge, hulking shape passing by—a giant slouching shadow deep in the fog. My heart pounded. The monster seemed to grumble to itself as it trudged toward the trash cans.

Riley stood up. I quickly scrambled to my feet as well.

I heard a trash-can lid hit the ground. I heard trash dumping out. I heard a loud thump and the sound of an empty trash can rolling away across the ground.

I stood frozen. And then I felt two hands pushing me toward the sounds. "Stop it," I whispered. "Don't push."

"We've got to get closer," Riley's voice insisted. "We've got to get its picture."

I leaned my weight back, but Riley was bigger, and with each push I lost ground. The two of us stumbled closer to the noise. In a few seconds, I could see the faint outline of a huge, hairy creature bent over the trash, eating noisily.

"A little closer," Riley whispered and pushed me again. I stumbled forward another step and then refused to budge.

"OK, OK," I whispered. "No closer."

"Take the picture," Riley hissed in my ear.

With shaky hands I raised the camera to my face. I peered through the viewfinder at the huge dark shape in the mist. The sounds of eating stopped. A deep rumbling growl filled the air. It knew we were there! My knees went weak.

*"Now!"* Riley whispered. "Take the picture."

The huge creature rose up on its feet and towered above us. It growled. I squeezed the button on my camera just as the creature took a clumsy step toward us.

The flash lit up the scene like a bolt of lightning, and I saw it clearly—a tall, scrawny, almost hairless bear. It was reared up on its hind legs, raising its leathery paws above its head.

The forest plunged into darkness again—a deeper darkness now, because my eyes were blinded by the flash. I blinked, but the image of the bear seemed burned into my eyes. It roared and then I heard it pound across the ground in our direction.

I dropped the camera and took off running. I still couldn't see a thing, but I ran full tilt through the darkness, not caring what was ahead, as long as I kept away from what was behind!

Ahead of me I heard Riley sprinting through the underbrush yelling for help. I followed him, tripping and stumbling and plowing a crazy path through the brush—the bear pummeling the ground behind me. The fog swirled all around me, but I managed to get close enough to Riley to see him through the fog.

Suddenly, the construction site fence was in front of us. Riley made a turn and sprinted along the fence where the trees had been cleared. I followed. It was easier running along the level, clear ground—but I knew it was also easier for the bear. And I knew that even an old scrawny bear could run faster than a person! I could hear it gaining ground behind me. I pushed myself harder and gained some ground on Riley.

I don't know if he thought I was the bear closing in on him, but Riley picked up his pace and started pulling away from me. He'd always been a better athlete than me.

And then I saw it, ahead of us in the fog. A low branch jutting out from a tree that hadn't been felled when they'd cleared the construction site. The branch angled up and over the top of the fence. It was our only hope.

"The branch," I yelled. Before the words were out of my mouth, Riley leaped up and grabbed the branch. He swung himself up in one fluid motion and then scrambled along the branch till he disappeared on the other side of the fence.

It was my turn. The branch was over my head now, and I could feel the bear tearing up the ground, coming closer to my heels with every stride. I'd never been much of an athlete, but I'd also never been so motivated!

I leaped as high in the air as I could. One hand gripped the branch, the other hand slipped. I kicked at the air with my legs, just as the snarling bear arrived on the spot. I pulled myself up and scrambled along the branch in a panic until I was on the other side of the construction site fence.

"Jump down," Riley's voice called to me from down on the ground. I swung down from the branch and then dropped to the ground.

Riley laughed. "We made it!" he puffed. "We made it!" Although he was breathless from running, he did a little victory dance. I scrambled to my feet and dusted myself off.

"I thought we were goners for sure," Riley said. "But we're safe now."

I put my hands on my knees and bent over to catch my breath. Relieved as I was, I felt like throwing up.

"We're safe!" Riley said again.

I heard a groaning behind me. But it wasn't the groaning of a frustrated bear, it was the groaning of plywood bending and nails being pulled out.

I glanced behind me and saw a huge section of the fence slowly topple away. The bear had torn it loose.

I took off running again. This time I was in the lead. I sprinted deep into the construction site, among stacks of lumber and mounds of bricks. I dodged this way and that, around buildings and bulldozers, with Riley on my heels.

And then I saw something strange. Although the ground had been perfectly level when the fence was built around the site, a mountain now loomed before me in the fog. I didn't stop to wonder. I just started climbing. I scrambled over boulders and scuttled along ledges, working higher and higher, never looking back. I climbed and climbed until I collapsed, exhausted, on a high ledge.

I heard something coming up behind me—it might have been the bear, it might have been Riley. I didn't care. I could go no farther. I just lay there waiting, my chest heaving, my heart pounding.

In a moment a shape rose up on the ledge beside me. I squeezed my eyes shut.

"Dude, where *are* we?" It was Riley. I smiled. I couldn't answer. I couldn't breathe. But I smiled.

Riley sat down next to me. "That's one angry bear," he said. "But it's still down there on the ground. What do you say we stay up here for a while?"

I lifted my head off the ledge and looked at Riley. "If you insist," I gasped, and let my head fall back.

# Chapter 10

The next thing I knew, it was morning. I opened my eyes and looked up at a bright blue sky. A banner flapped above my head in the breeze. Riley snored next to me. We seemed to be lying on some kind of railroad track. I struggled to sit up, sore and exhausted. I heard a voice down below us—a voice that echoed oddly.

I dragged myself to the edge of the ledge and looked down. I couldn't believe how high we were. How did we manage to get up here? How would we ever get down? Far below me was a grandstand full of people and a bunch of news vans. The town fire truck was parked alongside the grandstand. What was going on here? I glanced over my shoulder at Riley. He lay on his back, snoring away.

I shaded my eyes with my hand and squinted up at the banner stretched above our heads: BIGFOOT MOUNTAIN ROLLER COASTER.

My mind started to put things together. Piece after piece fell into place. It all started to make sense. They were building an amusement park. This was the grand unveiling of the first attraction—and we were sitting on it!

I peeked over the edge again. Mayor Pickett stood in front of the grandstand talking into a microphone. A brass band stood by. Banners and streamers were strung up everywhere. About a dozen news cameras pointed at the mayor.

I pushed myself back from the edge and shook Riley.

"Quit it," he mumbled and rolled over.

I shook him again. He opened his eyes and sat up groggily.

"Where am I?"

"We're at the grand unveiling of the Bigfoot Mountain Roller Coaster," I told him. "And unfortunately, I think we have the best seats in the house."

"Huh?"

"We've been duped," I told him. "I'll bet the skeleton was planted. The footprint was probably fake. It was all one of Mayor Pickett's publicity stunts. He wanted to get some free publicity, and we played right into his hands. It's just a stupid roller coaster. See for yourself."

Riley read the banner stretched above us. He looked at me and then crawled over to the edge of the ledge. He looked down at the crowd. Mayor Pickett's voice echoed on the loudspeakers, but I couldn't make out what he was saying. Riley scratched his head.

"You mean there wasn't any Bigfoot?" he said.

"Nope. Just two idiots and one scrawny bear that came down from the mountains to scrounge for trash."

The news didn't seem to disappoint Riley much. "Oh well," he said. "At least we get to be on TV." He stood up and started waving down at the grandstand.

Mayor Pickett's voice suddenly stopped, and a murmur arose from the crowd. Riley cupped his hands around his mouth to make a megaphone. "Can someone help get us down?" he yelled. "We're stuck."

I groaned and stood up next to Riley. When I looked down, all the news cameras were pointed at us. Riley grinned and waved. "Little help?" he shouted.

If Mayor Pickett had any plans for continuing his speech, no one seemed to care. All we could hear from our vantage point was loud laughter and people talking. All eyes were on us, and no one was paying attention to the mayor. The news cameras moved in to get a better picture of us. The red-faced mayor gave up trying to finish his speech and twisted to look up at us. "You two come down off of there!" his voice echoed in the loudspeakers. "You're disrupting the Grand Opening."

Riley scratched the back of his head and then made his hands into a megaphone again. "I suppose we could wait," Riley yelled. "How long you planning to take?"

The mayor said something into the microphone, but I couldn't hear because of all the laughter. A man in a suit climbed up on the podium and whispered something urgently into Mayor Pickett's ear. The mayor covered the microphone with his hand and the two of them argued a few moments. Finally the mayor nodded his head.

The volunteer firemen sprang into action and started the fire truck. They were only about fifty feet from the roller coaster, but for some reason they put on the siren and all the flashing lights—I suppose it was because of all the cameras. It took them a few minutes to back the fire truck up to the Bigfoot Mountain Roller Coaster and raise the ladder.

I looked down at all the cameras. We'd probably end up on every newscast in the state—at the very end, when they have dumb clips of dogs that water-ski or people who find a moose in their kitchen.

The extension ladder on the back of the fire truck pivoted around and slowly stretched up toward us. A fireman wearing a yellow helmet rode at the top of the ladder in a thing that looked like a giant red bucket. When it got close, Riley told me to go first. He seemed in no hurry to go down to face the mayor.

When the big bucket was close enough, the fireman tossed me a leather harness and told me how to put it on. He clipped the other end to a bar welded inside the bucket and then helped me climb in. There was a wheezing sound, and we started the slow descent. I looked up at Riley, who appeared to be rising up into the sky.

When we reached the ground, I climbed out of the bucket and was greeted by loud applause and a few cheers. I looked out at the people in the grandstand; I didn't see anyone from town. Cameras flashed in my eyes.

The rescue ladder wheezed and started to rise again. The mayor rushed over to me—I thought he wanted to see if I was OK, but he was just trying to be included in the pictures the reporters were taking. He pushed in next to me and put his hand on my shoulder.

"It was all a publicity stunt, wasn't it?" I asked him. "The skeleton. The footprint. You had us scared to death. You humiliated us in front of the whole school. You almost got us killed by a bear."

"Listen, kid," he said so only I could hear. "If it wasn't for the skeleton last month, these people wouldn't be out here now." He gestured over at the news vans and all the photographers. "All I had to do was call and say there was a new Bigfoot, and they all came running."

I didn't know what to say. I just shook my head. The mayor seemed awfully proud of himself, but the whole thing seemed pretty dishonest to me.

The ladder returned to the ground again and Riley hopped off. When he saw the mayor standing there smiling, with his hand on my shoulder, Riley grinned. He wasn't in trouble after all. Riley came and stood next to me. The cameras started flashing again.

"This was all the mayor's doing," I told Riley. "He planted the skeleton so all the news reporters would show up today. He *used* us."

Riley looked up at the mayor. "Very uncool," he said.

The mayor started to say something, but he was drowned out by the reporters, who started shouting questions.

"How did you boys end up up there?" one reporter shouted.

"We climbed up last night," Riley told them. "We got chased up there by a bear."

The reporter looked up to the high ledge we'd just come down from. "You climbed up *there?*" he asked us, amazed. "You're lucky you didn't break your neck."

"We weren't afraid," Riley told him. "'The Lord himself goes before you and will be with you; he will never leave you nor forsake you. Do not be afraid; do not be discouraged.' That's from the Bible."

"*Deuteronomy,*" I whispered to Riley. I was impressed that he remembered the verse.

"*Tudor on me,*" Riley told the reporter.

"Aren't you Sigmund Grump?" another voice asked. "Aren't you one of the boys who found the skeleton?"

"Well, sort of," Riley said. "It's a long story."

Eventually, the whole, long story came out. The reporters weren't pleased that they had been taken in by Mayor Pickett.

"Put the boys up on the podium," someone yelled. "Let's get one of them in front of the roller coaster."

In a few seconds, Riley and I were pushed up onto the mayor's podium. I looked out at all the cameras pointed at us. There was a sea of faces turned up toward us.

"This sure isn't how one of your dumb movies would have ended," I whispered to Riley.

"No," Riley said, mugging for the cameras, "but if they did make a movie out of this, I've got the perfect title."

Shutters clicked and cameras flashed, and Riley turned his attention back to grinning like a big fool.

"So what's your title?" I asked. I had a feeling I didn't want to know. Riley put his hands up like he was framing the screen of a movie theater. "How about *Wild Ride on Bigfoot Mountain?*"

I looked out at the cameras and the grandstand full of laughing people.

"It'll do," I told Riley. "It'll do."


An hour later, Riley and I hiked along the construction site fence toward my house.

"So, you think I can go with you again next week?" Riley asked.

I had no idea what he was talking about. "Go where?"

"Sunday school," he said.

I grinned at him. "Of course you can," I told him. "You can even eat lunch with us afterward."

"Good," Riley said. "Because I've been reading ahead, and I want to hear more about that monster Goliath—you ever heard of him?"

I grinned. "Yeah," I said. "I've heard of him, but he's not a monster."

"Are you kidding?" Riley said. "Haven't you ever seen *Canyon of the Giants?*"

"That's just a movie," I told him. I didn't like the direction this conversation was taking.

"Yeah," Riley said. "But the Bible's true—so giants were real. Right?"

I sighed. "Sure," I told him. "But—"

"Maybe some of them survived," Riley said, wide eyed. "If they did, I bet they'd be hiding someplace deep in the woods where no one could find them."

I looked over at Riley and blinked. Hadn't he learned *anything* from all this? "Giants?" I said. "In McCreeville?"

Riley grinned. "You never know," he told me. "You never know."

Don't miss another exciting

# HEEBIE JEEBIES

adventure!


Turn the page for an exciting chapter from

# THE I SCREAM TRUCK

# Chapter 1

U nbelievable. Alone in a cemetery at dusk. I scanned the headstones that cluttered the green hills. Not a soul in sight. They were gone. All of them. Gone.

"Dad?" I called out. Dead silence. "Mom?"

My parents had abandoned me. Or maybe the graves had swallowed them alive.

Mentally, I retraced our steps. First, we laid my great uncle to rest. Then we meandered from plot to plot to pay our respects to the rest of the dearly departed McAllister clan. The historic cemetery dated back to colonial times. The headstones resembled granite monuments, some taller than a coffin on end.

The McAllister graves were grouped according to family, but spread out in different sections of the cemetery. For some reason, my parents were reluctant to go along at first, but finally conceded. We plodded up one hill, then down another. We stayed within sight of each other, sometimes gathering at a single grave to share memories. My dad was right behind me just seconds ago. At least it seemed like seconds.

Now my nearest company was a marble headstone the size of a freezer. The engraved letters offered a tribute to the kid below.

JACOB ROBIN MCALLISTER
Born - February 13, 1927
Died - January 24, 1940
*Already Home*

I did the math. Jacob was twelve when he died, nearly thirteen. Same age as me.

A coyote howled nearby. A bat swooped low.

I formed a megaphone with my hands and shouted. "Mom? Dad?"

Silence answered. Nothing more.

I returned my attention to Jacob's white memorial. What I did next might have been disrespectful, but I figured a twelve-year-old kid would understand, especially a relative. Taking my best leap upward, I scaled the imposing monument. The marble felt cool against my hands as I pulled myself up. I brought my knee to the top of the headstone.

From there I rose to my feet and searched all around. No parents. No groundskeeper. No one. Just the silver slice of moon to light the night. A sudden gust whipped my back. I extended my hands to keep my balance and for a second it looked like I was trying to surf the tomb.

I couldn't believe it. What kind of parents would ditch their only child in a cemetery? I'd have to find my way back, alone. Then they'd probably blame me for making *them* wait. I could just hear my dad now: "Where have you been?" he would say from the front seat of the car.

Peering down through the gathering darkness for a soft place to land, I jumped to the ground. I landed wrong and twisted my ankle. "Ye-ouch!" I grimaced, trying to walk it off. That didn't help. I had definitely sprained it. The long walk to the car just got longer. I limped up the hill. My ankle felt like it was in a vise. Each step was torture. I had no choice but to take my time.

Then a leaf crunched nearby.

I spun around. Grim headstones stared back. I spoke to all of them at once, thinking I had figured it out. "Funny. You can come out now."

The mystery person gave me the silent treatment. "Dad? Mom?"

Not a word.

Another yelp from the coyote. A firefly flickered in my peripheral vision, then vanished.

Now what? My ankle hurt too much to play tombstone tag with the person hiding from me. I decided on a rational approach. I spoke to the black marble tower two rows down. "I know you're there. You might as well show yourself. Joke's over."

No answer.

*Enough already.* I tightened my stomach, determined not to flinch when whoever-it-was jumped out to scare me. I wouldn't give him the satisfaction. The top of the hill wasn't getting any closer, so I started off again, shifting into an urgent limp.

Leaves crunched. I didn't turn. More crunching. It had to be footsteps. I gave in and jerked my head around. A shoulder disappeared behind a broad headstone—at least it looked like a shoulder. "Real funny. You're caught. Just come out already."

No one did.

I debated. I wanted to go on the counter-offensive and scare the heebie jeebies out of the pain-in-the-neck who was trying to scare me. But with my clumsy ankle, I knew he would hear me coming. Besides, I still didn't know *who* I was dealing with. The funeral and graveside service had attracted weird relatives by the dozen. Aunt Gwen, who resembled a bag lady. Great Grandpa Fred, whose teeth rivaled Dracula's. But at least I knew who *they* were. Others I'd never seen before. One guy reminded me of a designer pirate. He wore a gold hoop earring, black eye patch, and double-breasted suit. What's worse, it had seemed like every-one was looking at me—including Captain Crook.

"How are you handling all of this?" my aunt had asked as soon as the service ended.

I told her "fine," since I hardly knew my great uncle.

"You're sure?" my aunt replied, unconvinced.

At that point, I was ready to get away from the McAllister clan—at least those still among the living. Even as I wove through the tombstones with my parents, I could see my relatives watching me.

The top of the hill drew near. I hobbled ahead, certain of one thing: a graveyard is no place for wimps—not at night, anyway. The footsteps behind me grew louder. Now, instead of one person, it sounded like two. My ankle throbbed against my shoe. But I pressed on. Just a few more feet. Steps trampled the grass in my wake, drawing closer.

I made it! I crested the hill. I could see our car in the distance, parked in dark solitude. The only one left in the lot. I watched the front windshield for movement inside. No one stirred.

It occurred to me that if my parents *were* in the car, whoever was following me might not be playing a joke at all. My heart pounded. I drew quick, short breaths. I kicked into a limp-jog. The sounds behind me faded, but I kept up the pace. I wove through the gravestones like an injured running back. I crossed rows of graves. Fifty feet to the car. Forty. I was making too much noise to hear anyone's footsteps but my own.

Thirty more feet. Twenty. I extended my stride. Almost there.

"You!" a raspy voice warned. "Stop! Now!"

I didn't even slow down. Ten feet from the car, I glanced back. Two fierce eyes, like infrared beams, bored into mine. A crooked finger pointed at my head. But it was the shovel that caught my attention. The angry-looking man carried it like an ax. I stumbled backward toward the car.

When my hand touched the cold metal of the back door, I grabbed the handle and yanked. It lifted, but nothing happened. Locked. I pounded on the glass. My heart went berserk against my chest.

"Mom? Dad? Hit the unlock button!"

I listened for the familiar *click*.

No click. The tinted windows did their job. I couldn't see whether anyone was in there.

The old man marched toward me. He stared me down. "What did I tell you?" he asked, knowing I knew the answer.

I slapped the back window. *Thump! Thump! Thump!* I cupped my hands against the front windshield. My mom and dad were in there, but not moving.

"Mom! Dad!" I wailed.

The raspy voice. The crooked finger. The shovel! Twelve feet and closing.

I tried the back door again. Still locked. I pounded on the glass, performing CPR on our dead car.

*Click.* Finally!

I jerked open the back door, but froze. I didn't jump inside. I couldn't. The face staring back at me was twice as scary as the one in pursuit.